THE MARQUESS'S STOLEN BRIDE

Dukes Gone Dirty
Book 3

Bella Moxie

ARE YOU SIGNED UP FOR DRAGONBLADE'S BLOG?

You'll get the latest news and information on exclusive giveaways, exclusive excerpts, coming releases, sales, free books, cover reveals and more.

Check out our complete list of authors, too!

No spam, no junk. That's a promise!

Sign Up Here

www.dragonbladepublishing.com

Dearest Reader;

Thank you for your support of a small press. At Dragonblade Publishing, we strive to bring you the highest quality Historical Romance from some of the best authors in the business. Without your support, there is no 'us', so we sincerely hope you adore these stories and find some new favorite authors along the way.

Happy Reading!

CEO, Dragonblade Publishing

CHAPTER ONE

MADELINE RACED UP the circular staircase, barefoot and trembling.

Her hands shook as she wrapped her night-rail tightly around her, her fingers fumbling to tie it shut.

Her heart pounded in sync with her bare feet as she made her way back to the safety of her room. She paused on the third-floor landing to catch her breath.

This was a mistake.

The moment she stopped running, her legs began to tremble and her stomach heaved. Clapping a hand over her mouth, she closed her eyes tightly and forced herself to breathe.

Resting against a wall, she drew in one shaky breath after another, trying not to hear the voices still coming from the parlor below. Male voices that would haunt her dreams.

"Let's have a look at her, then," the one with the oily beard had said to her mother. "I don't buy any property without having a good look."

She squeezed her eyes tight, but it didn't stop the tears from spilling down her cheeks.

Humiliation. Rage. Her whole body shook with it.

A sound came from one of the bedrooms to her left.

Her father was in his rooms. Likely in bed. Maybe asleep. She'd like to think he had no idea what his wife was doing while he was ill. Highly possible.

According to the doctors, he was not aware of much these days.

But if he were, would he have put a stop to it?

She squeezed her eyes shut. Possibly.

Perhaps.

She shook her head as a sob threatened to escape. What did it matter?

Her brother, Albert, had told her on his last visit that it was only a matter of time before their father passed away. And then what? Then Albert would be the new earl, and she'd be under his protection.

Albert would take care of her. If he had any idea what his mother was doing to her, he'd have put an end to it. And when he returned, he would save her.

The thought gave her hope. Enough that she was able to make her way to the narrow stone steps that led to her room in the drafty old turret.

The thick oak door to her room was open, but it would be locked up tight soon enough.

Her shaky legs gave way as she reached the bed in the middle of the room. The lone piece of furniture aside from a rickety old armoire.

Her fingers were cold as ice as she clutched at the opening of her nightdress, a shudder racking through her. She bit her lip to hold back a sob. She bit so hard, that she tasted blood, but it did not stop a choking noise from escaping her lips.

How had her life come to this?

But then again, perhaps this was always to be her fate. She shut her eyes with a wretched sigh. Perhaps she'd always been destined to have a tragic end. The bastard daughter of a mad earl?

What more could she expect?

Is he truly mad? she'd once asked Albert.

He'd been twelve and she, eight. She'd overheard the servants whispering. It was the first hint she'd received that perhaps her life was not normal. That to the rest of the world, her father was known to be mad, and she…

Well, she'd find out soon enough that she didn't exist—as far as the rest of the world was concerned.

But mad or not, it wasn't her father who was tormenting her now. It was her mother.

Well, the closest thing she had to a mother. The woman who'd raised her.

The countess was getting desperate.

Madeline had watched her descend into…what?

Madness? Hardly. The older woman was cunning and cruel, but she had her wits about her. And she knew the end of her reign was near. With the earl at death's door and her son grown, she'd be the dowager countess soon enough.

All those years of cruelty were catching up with her.

Her own son despised her, and her father's horrid rulership had left the earldom destitute. Soon there would be nothing left for the countess.

Madeline looked down at her bare feet, frigid against the stone floor.

Was it any wonder the countess had taken desperate actions? No one should have been surprised, least of all Madeline.

And yet, her mind still reeled at the low depths to which her mother had sunk. Selling off her own daughter. Letting those men see her. Touch her…

A scratching noise from outside her tower window had her glancing over, but then it stopped.

The wind, no doubt. Perhaps the scraping of branches from one of the nearby trees.

She drew in a deep breath. *Think*, she ordered her rattled brain.

She needed to think.

She had no time to lose.

When Albert took over, she would be safe. But when would he return?

Her tongue probed at the bite mark on her lip.

Tonight was just the beginning. She flinched at the memory of her mother's cold smirk and soulless eyes as she'd stood back and let those men order Madeline about.

No, not her mother.

For years she'd clung to that name because her father told her to call his wife that. Who he thought they were fooling was anyone's guess. Madeline's dark hair and skin were a dead giveaway that she'd not been born to the countess.

And tonight had proved once again that no matter what connection they shared through her father and Albert, the countess would never be her mother.

Tonight had made it clear that the woman who'd raised her was out for blood.

Well, riches. But she'd sacrifice whatever it took to get it.

Including Madeline.

Madeline was up and off the bed, on her knees seeking out the small box of treasures she had stored there when she heard it again. Another scratching sound outside the window.

She pulled out the box and opened it to find all her worldly possessions. A meager collection, no doubt. But the trinkets and money were hers. Her fingers ran over the coins she'd managed to steal over the years. Again…a small amount. But it would have to do.

She set the box down on the bed and stood.

Was she really going to do this?

She let out a long breath as she glanced toward the still-open door. Yes. She had to. There was no telling when Albert would return from his latest sojourn. The earl had sent him off on a trip to handle the earldom's finances and manage their estates. No easy task considering the way it had been mismanaged over the years.

Even if she knew precisely where he was and found a way to get a letter to him this very day, there was no way to know if he'd arrive back here in time to save her.

Her gaze flickered to the window again when she heard a loud thump.

She shook her head. What was going on out there?

Didn't matter. What mattered was that her door was open now and it wouldn't be for much longer. This could be her one opportunity to escape.

She paced the confines of her small bedroom. Prison, more like. Albert had explained to her long ago that most girls were not kept locked away like an animal. She knew that it was odd, and she knew it was something straight out of one of those story-books Albert used to read to her.

But that was their father's way. He had a flair for the melodramatic. A power-hungry need to control everyone he was responsible for. And as his health declined, his ideas of how he ought to protect his family grew more and more outlandish.

She'd heard whispers of duels. Murders, even. All committed in his name over whatever slight he believed was done against him.

They'd all suffered his fickle temper, perhaps none more so than the countess. But whatever it was that had driven him to fits of rage and long bouts of melancholy, it had him lying on his deathbed now.

Not even he could save her.

Her heart gave a jolt of alarm as another noise cut through the silence. This time it was difficult to say if it came from outside or belowstairs. What if the countess had sent a servant up to lock her in?

Oh no, she must not dally if she were to take advantage of the unlocked door.

She headed to the armoire. Clothes. She'd need to be properly dressed if she were to make a run for it tonight, and she had to hurry.

Sounds from outside her window distracted her from her task, and it took longer than it ought to find her darkest most functional gown and cast it onto the bed.

She had to disrobe, but stupidly, her fingers weren't working. They trembled when she tried to untie the sash that held her clothes together. Her skin crawled with the memories of those lecherous beasts below grasping at her, jeering at her…

She cursed her own weakness.

There would be time to weep later. But for now, her time was running out.

A loud crash outside her window had her scrambling over to look, but all she could see was darkness on this cloudy, moonless night.

There was nothing out there but the wind and the trees. And if there was any foolish, girlish hope still left in her that some knight would come to her rescue, surely, they'd died this very night.

CHAPTER TWO

WYATT DRUTHERS, THE fifth Marquess of Hayden, had done many foolish things in his lifetime. Nearly all of them when he was in his cups.

But as he lay on the cold, wet lawn before an old, crumbling stone house on the outskirts of London, he stared up through the bare trees at a dark sky and wondered.

Was this the most foolish of them all?

The shock of this latest fall faded, and he groaned as the pain set in.

Yes. Undoubtedly, yes.

This was far and away the most foolish quest he'd ever set out on. It put Quixote to shame. His friend Malcolm's face appeared above his. "Ready to call an end to this idiotic mission?"

It had all started with a farfetched tale at their friend Benedict's wedding. Hayden had said that he'd met every marriageable young lady in London, and someone else—who was it? They'd said, nay. Not every lady. And that was the first he'd heard of the mythical daughter of the legendary mad earl.

"Can you not just admit that it's a silly tall tale?" Malcolm asked, his tone weary with exhaustion. "Just pay the fools who took the bet and let's get home to bed."

Hayden waved aside the suggestion. He never gave up, not when his pride was at stake. He and his friends had gone to

Vestry Lane to gamble and drink, and he'd opened his big mouth…and next thing Hayden knew, the betting had begun.

He held up a hand, which Malcolm grabbed, helping to hoist him upright. Again.

Turrets, he'd discovered, were bloody hard to climb. Even harder when they were crumbling and ancient.

"My pride is on the line, Malcolm." He brushed off his trousers as he gazed up at the dark window of the turret above. "I shall not stop until I've proven whether this girl is fact or fiction."

"Mmm." Malcolm crossed his arms and regarded him with wry amusement. "And what precisely is the point of this mission, Don Quixote?"

"The point is to save her," he said, pointing upward.

"If she exists," Malcolm added.

"Right. If she's real, she ought to be saved." Hayden tried to focus on Malcolm, but the world was spinning.

He narrowed his eyes and peered up at the stones he'd just slid down. Perhaps now was not the best time to be scaling a tower wall. But he'd never been one to back down from a wager before.

And truth be told, he rather fancied the idea of being some lady's knight in shining armor.

Malcolm folded his arms and regarded him seriously. Which was not abnormal, really. Malcolm always had been serious, even before his father had died and he'd become the new Earl of Fallenmore.

"You're an earl now," Hayden felt the need to point out.

"Indeed I am." Malcolm's smile was tolerant. They'd gone back a long way, and Malcolm was used to Hayden's carousing.

"You and Benedict," he added. "Suddenly I have two earls in my circle of friends. Funny how that happened."

Malcolm arched a brow. "I wouldn't say 'funny' is the word for it."

"No, no, of course not." New titles only came about when death was at hand. So no, not very amusing, come to think of it.

Even so, he found himself sitting in the wet grass musing over how much had befallen his friends of late. Two earls and a duke…and lastly him, the marquess. It'd been just the four of them for an age, and perhaps that was the trouble.

They were all so bloody fortunate. They'd all had everything handed to them.

And he'd watched each of his friends find love in the same way. Oh, maybe not *handed* to them. They'd had some struggles along the way. But the right woman had been so obvious. Benedict had found his equal in Philippa, with her brazen spirit and her fierce temper. Raff had found someone to soften his hard edges in the sweet and angelic Evangeline. And Malcolm had managed to come to peace with his unfortunate past when he'd found his Vivian.

But Hayden couldn't expect the same good fortune. As he'd claimed at Benedict's wedding, and which had set tonight's adventure into motion—he'd met every pretty young chit good society had to offer.

He squinted up at the dark window at the top. Unless this one was real. And that was highly questionable.

He thought he caught a glimmer of…something in the window. There and gone so fast it made his head spin.

He groaned as the world truly did begin to spin.

It was either the scotch or the fall that had addled his head. Or perhaps both.

He sat back down with a thud. Just until the world stopped spinning. Then he'd try again.

"Look, Hayden, I came with you this far to try and keep you from doing something stupid." Malcolm glanced at the wall and back down at him. "Something even more stupid than you've just done."

"Yes, yes. Poor judgment. I've heard it all my life," he muttered.

But it hadn't stopped anyone from handing him the marquessate after his father died, and it didn't seem to deter any of the marriage-minded mothers who kept thrusting young ladies into his path as if he might be tripped and felled into the marriage bed.

Hayden knew what was expected of him—and he'd do it. But he'd do it on his terms, and not to one of those manipulative little minxes who thought to seduce him, or those sweet innocent little virgins who hadn't the faintest notion *how* to seduce him.

Was he too particular?

Perhaps.

"Come on, Hayden, I'll get you home," Malcolm said.

Hayden jabbed a finger up toward Malcolm's stern face. "You just want to get home to your wife."

Malcolm smirked. "Can you blame me?"

Hayden grunted. No. He couldn't. Malcolm's wife, Vivian, was lovely in the extreme. As were Benedict's wife and Raff's. Each woman was so very different, and yet so very well suited to each of his friends.

He found himself scowling down at the ground.

"You jealous, old chum?" Malcolm asked with a wry grin. "If so, you know there are plenty of women—"

"Not jealous," he muttered. "And I'll choose a wife when I'm good and ready. But first…" He moved his pointer finger upward toward the alleged prison. "I must save the princess."

"She's not a princess," Malcolm pointed out. "And no one truly expects you to save anyone."

He had to struggle to sit upright again. Malcolm's words lit a fire. No, of course, no one expected that of him. And that was precisely the challenge he needed to forge ahead.

No one expected him to win this, eh?

Well. He'd show them.

He stumbled a few times as he got back to his feet, but he threw himself back upon that stone wall with a vengeance.

Malcolm sighed behind him. "I'm leaving you here if you don't come with me now."

"Fine, go," Hayden grunted.

"Don't do anything foolish…" Malcolm trailed off as he watched Hayden seek out a new foothold. "Oh, forget it. You've lost your bloody mind."

"Maybe," he bit out.

It was harder than one might expect to climb a wall, even one covered in ivy and trellises like this one. It was even harder to climb it while speaking. And swaying.

Wait a moment. Was he swaying or was the tower shifting beneath his weight?

Bloody hell. He really shouldn't have had that last drink.

He lost his footing, and he heard something tumble to the ground below.

"For the love of God, Malcolm. Benedict and Raff will kill me if you die on my watch."

Hayden gave an appreciative snort of laughter. "Nonsense. They'd never blame you. Not after all the trouble I gave them over the years."

Malcolm sighed. "That's not the point."

"What is the point then?" Oh hell, he was already breathing hard. Climbing a wall was much harder than he'd been led to believe.

"The point is I'd rather you didn't die."

"We're all going to die, Malcolm. And if I die here tonight, let it be known that I did it for the sake of honor and duty and—*oof*."

"Hayden?"

"I'm fine. I'm all right." He found a ledge to rest on. That had been a close call there.

"You do realize that this whole lady-in-a-tower story is likely just that, don't you? A story?"

Hayden grunted. He was rather counting on it. He hadn't the slightest idea what to do with a damsel in distress if he were to come upon one. But then again…there was something rather poetic and chivalrous about finding some poor lass who'd been locked away by a mad king—er, earl.

Whatever.

"It's all just whispers," Malcolm continued. "No one's ever seen a daughter."

Hayden was only half listening. His gaze was narrowed on the next climb ahead of him.

"Surely if the mad earl had some beautiful daughter, he'd be trying to marry her off. Everyone knows he hasn't a coin left to his name."

"Mmph," Hayden grunted. They'd been through all this before. Malcolm had spent the better half of the carriage ride here trying to convince him to turn back from his foolish quest.

"These rumors about her being some great beauty?" Malcolm continued with a scoff of disdain. "The tales of her being captive? And in a tower, of all things? Can't you see some nitwit has been spinning a yarn, that's all."

"Perhaps," Hayden agreed. "But we're here now, aren't we? And look…" He turned to grin at his friend and nearly lost his grip. "I'm halfway there."

"And then what?" Malcolm muttered. "What would you do if you found some young lady up there? Marry her?"

Hayden chuckled. "I doubt it'll come to that, Malcolm."

"If you want to be a hero, help me take down Vivian's louse of a father. Or better yet, vanquish this world of that no-good Foley."

Hayden growled at the mention of the weasel who'd been wreaking havoc on their lives of late. First, he'd preyed upon Raff's wife and then Benedict's. The man was a bottom-feeding scavenger just looking for weaknesses to exploit so he could win a fortune or some power.

Pathetic.

"Says the man who's climbing a stone wall just to win a dare," he muttered to himself.

"What was that?" Malcolm responded.

"Nothing. Never mind."

Malcolm raised his voice slightly to be heard. "I'm telling you, if you get caught by the earl—"

"I'll only be caught if you keep shouting," Hayden hissed.

Malcolm's sigh was nearly as loud as his talking.

"Almost there," Hayden muttered. His fingers grasped for the window's edge. There was candlelight flickering within.

Someone *was* in there.

His insides gave a jolt of awareness, some of the drunken haze lifting with this rush of alertness.

The rumors couldn't be true…

Could they?

No. No, of course not. This was likely just a servant's room, or a nursemaid, or—

He heaved himself up and over the edge, the window swinging inward with a crash. He tumbled inside just as someone screamed.

A girl.

He sat up. Nay, a lady.

His gaze caught on the nearly naked figure who hovered next to the bed with a hand to her mouth and her eyes wide with terror.

Wrong again. This was not merely a lady.

His heart did a leap before diving off a cliff as her fear-stricken eyes met his.

This was the most beautiful woman he'd ever seen.

CHAPTER THREE

MADELINE COULDN'T FIND words. "What are you…who are you…where…?" Her gaze went from the ridiculously handsome man suddenly seated on her floor to the window through which he'd so dramatically appeared.

"I will scream," she said.

At the same time, he said, "I'm here to save you."

They both went silent.

"You're here to…what?" She blinked and stared as if maybe that might help her mind comprehend this turn of events.

Fear took hold as a new idea came to her. "Are you one of…one of *them*?"

One of the men her mother was attempting to sell her off to, she meant. One of the buyers, the countess had called them.

As if she were a horse or some cattle.

But he looked nearly as stunned as she felt to find her here. And he didn't look cruel like the others had.

Not that looks had anything to do with it, but even so…

There was nothing frightening about the way he was eyeing her. Though his eyes did grow dark as he took her in—

"Oh, good heavens," she hissed. In her shock, she'd forgotten she'd been in the middle of changing. With quick movements, she threw on the night-rail she'd only just discarded.

"Who are you?" she tried again. Her heart was pounding hard

in her throat, and she was tempted to scream for help again.

She might have if she believed there was a single soul in this house who'd protect her.

The man ignored her question, throwing his own out instead. "Are you…her? Are you the mad earl's daughter?"

She straightened, pride and anger churning in her gut. "Who are you, and why did you just crash in through my window?"

He scrambled to his feet. "We heard…that is, I'd heard…" He shook his head, and she frowned.

"Are you…" She recoiled as he drew near. Not because he was so very frightening—he was large, yes, but his face was that of an angel. He was like a prince from a storybook, not some brute of a criminal. But it was the stench rolling off of him that had her stepping back even further. "Are you drunk, sir?"

"Am I…" He laughed. "I suppose I am."

"You're a madman," she whispered.

Of course.

Of course, he was.

This was her lot in life. Clearly. She'd been raised by a madman, and now they were flocking in through her window like errant birds.

She shook her head, pointing to the still-open window. "Go. You must go before…" She turned at the sound of voices on the lower floor.

Had someone heard her scream?

"Go," she hissed. "Go before they find you."

Alarm lit his eyes, but something else as well. Something much more terrifying.

Something almost…noble.

"Who?" he demanded. His brows came down and that drunken daze seemed gone entirely as he took in her surroundings. It was a pitiful sight, to be certain. She practically felt the jolt when his gaze landed on the thick door with the bars and the key…on the outside.

"Are you a servant?" he asked.

"No."

His eyes met hers. "Are you a prisoner?"

Her eyes widened. Her mouth opened. *No. Say no.*

But she couldn't say it. All her life she'd told herself she wasn't. That she was hidden away for her protection like her father had said, no matter what Albert had told her.

But right now, she couldn't say no. Because…wasn't she trying to run away?

He straightened, and she could see him eyeing the door with purpose. Like he was about to burst through it and confront whoever he might find. "Your name, Miss."

"What? N-no." Without thinking she gripped his arm, as if she could hold him back. He looked down at where her hand rested on his forearm.

He wasn't wearing a jacket, and the fabric of his shirt was so thin, she could feel the heat from his skin.

"Tell me what is happening here," he demanded. "I swear to you, I am only here to help."

"To help…" Her eyes widened with new understanding. "Are you…did Albert send you?"

His confusion gave him away.

She took a step back. But if not sent by Albert, then how did he come to be here? It made no sense. "Who sent you? Why are you here?"

The voices were growing louder. He heard them now, too, she was certain, because they both cast panicked glances toward the door.

"Listen to me," he said. "I admit my intrusion was not well planned, but I came here with good intentions. Do you wish to stay here? Or do you want to leave?" He winced slightly, and a myriad of emotions seemed to pass through his eyes at once as he added, "With me."

"With…with you?" What did that mean?

The voices were growing ever nearer, and there was no place for him to hide.

Think, Madeline. She swallowed hard, her gaze landing on the box on her bed. All she owned, and she had no way of knowing how far it would get her, or if she would find safety along the way.

"Love..." He touched her chin, and his smile made the term of endearment feel heartachingly real.

Which was ridiculous. Obviously.

"I'm afraid I need an answer." He glanced meaningfully toward the door.

"If I go with you," she started.

She didn't know how to finish. This decision would change the rest of her life. Her entire future rested on what she said right now.

Because there was no denying the countess's voice from the staircase. She could put her faith in a stranger, whom she knew nothing about except for the fact that he was breathtakingly handsome and had for whatever reason broken into her tower room.

Or she could go along with the fate she knew.

"Yes, I'll go with you," she said.

He looked nearly as shocked as she felt, but he flashed her a charming grin as if she'd just said yes to tea and not...what?

Her heart leapt.

She had no idea.

What had she just said yes to? Who was he? What did he do? Why was he here? But most of all—

"Who are you?" The countess's high-pitched outrage had Madeline whirling around to face her.

Evil was beautiful. It sometimes shocked Madeline that this could be so. In the storybooks, evil looked evil and good looked good. But that wasn't the case in real life because the countess was stunning.

Tall, blonde, and with the sort of fine features that drove men to write poetry and carve statues. Or, in the case of her father...go mad.

"What is the meaning of this?" she hissed, her eyes wide with shock and rage.

Madeline opened her mouth but found herself blinking in shock as the newcomer beside her bowed low and gallant.

She blinked a few times and caught her mother doing the same.

One simply did not expect an intruder to bow.

"Pardon the intrusion, my lady," he said. And he winked.

The man winked.

Madeline now knew for certain that she was the one who'd lost her wits. Perhaps that was why they'd locked her in here all these years. Or maybe going mad was hereditary or—

Oh, what did it matter?

All that mattered was, delusion, dream, or reality, the most handsome man she'd ever seen was now striding toward her mother with a smile as that wretched Mr. Foley entered with several footmen.

The newcomer stopped short. "Foley."

It was said with a sneer, but after recovering from a moment of shock, Foley smirked. "My lord. What an unexpected turn of events."

"My lord?" The words slipped out before Madeline could stop them.

Her new protector—if that was indeed what he was—turned to her with a gentle smile that seemed utterly at odds with the sneer he'd worn when he'd first caught sight of Foley.

A sneer that was back in place as soon as he turned back.

"I should have known you'd be involved with this," the newcomer said to Foley. "Whatever this is."

Madeline's head whipped back and forth. What was she missing?

Foley's smirk made her cringe. He'd been downstairs before. He'd led those men in, he'd—

"I must admit," Foley said coolly. "You have me beat. You might have expected my presence, but I never would have imagined I'd find *you* here."

He chuckled as he held his hands out to encompass her cold, miserable chamber.

"Foley," the countess snapped. "What is the meaning of this? Who is this man?"

"My lady, allow me to introduce you to the Marquess of Hayden."

Madeline gasped and got another warm smile in return. What the…

"Marquess?" The countess looked wary. A sight Madeline had never seen before, and it had Madeline shifting closer to the newcomer.

Any man who could make the countess second guess herself was an ally. Of this she was certain.

Or…she was almost certain. Madeline glanced at…Hayden, was it? He was giving her an encouraging smile, reaching for her hand.

"Have you come for the auction?" the countess asked.

Ice slithered through Madeline's veins. *The auction.* That's what her mother was calling it? She wasn't even pretending it was anything other than it was.

She clutched at her night-rail—belatedly. Everyone in this room had already seen far too much of her.

She dipped her head, wishing she could disappear.

"The auction," Hayden repeated.

Madeline stiffened, her head snapping up to look between him and Foley and then to her mother. No. No! Surely not. He couldn't be one of them. She couldn't have just agreed to go off with another of her mother's buyers.

But Foley cut in, allaying that particular fear, at least.

"He was not invited here this evening, my lady. If I'm not mistaken, I believe his lordship was here to woo your daughter." He was eyeing Hayden with a knowing smirk that made her feel ill.

The countess frowned, and after a moment of indecision, she

seemed to decide that Foley was the safest bet to vent her frustration. "This will not do, Foley. You assured me you'd be bringing only those who would pay top dollar—"

"And he will, I am certain." Foley's gaze grew calculating.

Hayden's brows drew together. "Pay? For what? What is this auction—"

"Doesn't matter," Foley said. He drew her mother to the side and whispers began.

Hayden turned to her. "Auction?"

She shook her head as if she did not know. In truth, it was too demeaning to say aloud.

"Well," her mother finally said as she moved back toward them, her head held high and her tone genteel. "You must understand, my lord. We cannot have a gentleman alone in my daughter's room. My husband, God bless his soul, is not fit to defend her honor, but that does not mean—"

"No, of course," Hayden was saying. "You did not give me a chance to explain."

"Explain what?" the countess said.

Yes, explain what? Madeline had to bite her tongue to keep from echoing the question.

She had the horrible sensation that a pantomime was being performed all around her and she was the only one who hadn't read the script.

Everything about this was wrong, and yet everyone was acting like it was all right. Like this was how society conducted its affairs. In young ladies' bedrooms in the middle of the night.

"My apologies for alarming you," he said to the countess, but his gaze flickered over to Madeline. She saw a question there, and she nodded.

What was she agreeing to? She wasn't certain.

But did she have any choice?

"I ought to have announced myself properly," he was saying. And oh, his manners. His speech was fine and his smile so charming. "I was not certain if I ought to speak to your husband, your son, or you yourself, you see."

Her mother's smile reminded Madeline of a snake about to strike. "And what is your offer?"

"My offer?" He turned to her with a smile she couldn't match. "Why, it's marriage, of course. If she'll have me."

Madeline's lips parted but no sound came out.

What was happening?

This man didn't even know her. And he was a marquess. Why was he proposing marriage?

Because he has to, you ninny.

Some part of her mind was still able to reason. That part of her brain felt suddenly removed from the situation. Like there was some corner of her mind watching this entire scenario unfold from a distance.

Almost as if it were all happening to a stranger.

And so, yes, she could understand now why he'd so willingly go along with her mother's suggestion of marriage. It was either that or have his reputation destroyed and quite possibly die in a duel.

Marriage or death. And he'd chosen her.

She supposed she ought to be flattered that marriage to her was preferable to death.

Bitter humor made her lips twitch even as horror rose. Because the countess and this strange man were now making arrangements to meet again in the morning when they could discuss it properly.

Properly. As if anything about this was proper. Or even sane.

"We shall have to discuss the terms," the countess was saying. "But considering I found you alone in my daughter's room, I imagine you will be quite amenable to my offer."

It wasn't a question so much as a threat, but this blasted man—this marquess—smiled benignly as if this were all a common event for him. "Of course," he said.

He must be deep in his cups.

He reeked of liquor, certainly, but also that was the only

explanation for his easy demeanor in the face of this absurdity. The man had stumbled through her window, and now he was walking away engaged. To the mad earl's bastard daughter.

But for the love of God, why had he climbed into her room in the first place?

It seemed the countess shared her curiosity because she finally asked what Madeline had been dying to know. "Well, now that we've established that you'll be marrying my daughter just as soon as you're able, would you mind telling me just what you were doing in here?"

Her gaze was cold as ice as she shot a fierce glare in Madeline's direction.

Madeline shrank back, but then Hayden caught her hand in his and tugged until she was standing at his side.

Madeline blinked up at him in shock, but he was still smiling charmingly at the countess. "You see, my lady, there are rumors about that the mad—er, that is, the Earl of Ashburn has a daughter…"

The countess's lips curved into a sneer.

Madeline frowned. A rumor? Yes, her father had been over-protective and had kept her from society but…did truly *no one* outside these walls know that she was here?

To have this confirmed only solidified the hard knot in her chest. She'd been left here to rot, entirely at the countess's mercy, such as it was.

His grip tightened on her hand as he continued. "I'll admit, I'd thought it all a fantastical tale. After all, a sweet young damsel in distress locked away in a tower? Such a thing only happens in storybooks."

The countess's whole face was twitching with anger now.

"But here we are." He said it with a flippant air, yet Madeline could feel the shift in him. The crackle of energy and the new tension that had her holding her breath. Nervous, for some reason, but not on her own behalf.

It was the sensation that always happened before violence

broke out…

And Madeline knew it well.

She started to tremble, and that earned her a quick look of concern from Hayden before he turned back to face her mother, who was blustering through her rage.

"Those tales are ridiculous," she started.

"Are they?" His voice was so unnaturally calm, so terrifyingly gentle.

Her mother seemed to sense it, too, because she did not take the bait.

Mr. Foley, though, was foolish enough to step into the fray. "As you can see, my lord, the girl is alive and well."

Hayden barely acknowledged the gentleman who'd become her mother's eyes and ears in society. "Do not address me directly, Foley. Not if you wish to keep your life this evening."

Foley's lips curled in a sneer, but he took a step back in self-preservation.

"So, you came here," the countess said, waving toward the window. "You had the gall to break into my home to…what? See if the rumors were true?"

"I came here to save an innocent young lady," he said.

Oh dear. Madeline's legs trembled even more, but not out of fear. Something warm and sweet and completely unfamiliar unfurled in her chest and spread throughout her limbs.

"You came here looking to wed?" the countess scoffed.

"I came here to do whatever it took to save the girl. I have no objection to marriage."

That cut the countess down a notch, and Madeline felt a flicker of satisfaction seeing her mother's cold sneer falter.

His grip tightened on hers. She couldn't have escaped if she'd tried.

But she didn't try. Where would she go?

It was him on one side and her mother, who intended to sell her off, on the other.

Or you could run away, the voice of reason persisted.

Yes, she could at that.

But surely Hayden would not lock her away in a tower as well. She'd have time to formulate a plan, and—

"I came here to steal your daughter, if you must know."

She blinked up at him, that warm feeling fading fast. Steal her? Like she was a treasure chest or a pot of gold? She tugged on her hand, but he refused to let go.

"But you were caught," the countess taunted.

"Indeed. But that does not change my plan." He looked bored as he eyed the door behind them. "I'd prefer to leave by the front door, however, if it's all the same to you."

"What? You cannot—"

"I can, and I will take her with me when I leave," Hayden said. He eyed the countess and then Foley consideringly. "Unless you plan to stop me."

The countess gasped and sputtered, but Hayden turned to face Madeline with that charming, roguish grin that made her belly flutter. "My dear, is there anything you'd like to bring with you?"

For a moment, she froze.

This was happening.

She was leaving.

She couldn't breathe or think or react. Until he squeezed her hand. And that was the impetus she needed. "Just this," she whispered as she held up the small box. He took it from her and tucked it under his arm. "Allow me." He had to all but drag her toward the countess, who still blocked the door. Her feet and legs refused to work properly.

Madeline flinched away when they got close enough that the countess could strike.

But the countess ignored her and focused solely on the marquess who towered over her.

"What do you think you're doing?" she hissed.

"Simple." He grinned. "I'm stealing my bride."

CHAPTER FOUR

T HE EARL OF Foster was a stoic sort of man, so to see Benedict gaping and speechless was quite the sight. "So, to be clear…"

He paused, and Raff finished for him. "You're actually going to marry the girl."

The duke followed with an arch of his brows, his eyes filled with disbelief.

Hayden looked to Malcolm, who was slouched down in the armchair beside him, looking as exhausted as he felt. Malcolm shrugged.

Hayden glanced back to the two men who were standing in front of him…still gaping.

"I don't see that I have much of a choice, do you?" He'd meant for a jesting tone, but it merely sounded tired.

Because he *was* tired. He was so bloody tired.

He'd led his new fiancée—*fiancée!* He still couldn't quite believe it—down the stairs, to find Malcolm arguing with two footmen at the front door, demanding to be let in. He'd taken one look at Hayden, a longer, far more startled glance at the half-dressed beauty at his side, and had led the way back to his chaise.

On the ride back to Malcolm's home, they'd come up with a plan. A temporary fix, at least, as the poor girl had sat there staring at them in wide-eyed silence.

Malcolm had been shockingly sensible once he'd digested the fact that the lovely but unkempt woman in his carriage was to be Hayden's wife. They'd agreed Hayden couldn't take her to his home. Not yet. Not until they were married. Malcolm had offered to house her until then.

Through it all, his bride-to-be had remained silent except to answer when he asked her name, and again to confirm that she was, in fact, the earl's daughter.

The moment they'd arrived at Malcolm's townhome in Mayfair, Malcolm had called for Vivian, who'd come downstairs with her hair down and asking blessedly few questions. She'd taken one look at Madeline, tsked softly, and had used the gentlest voice Hayden had ever heard when she'd told Madeline to follow her to her new room.

He supposed she was there now. He'd heard servants bustling about and a bath being ordered…

It was the dead of night, but this household was alive with activity as they prepared for their new houseguest.

"I'm sorry to call you out of your beds at this hour," Hayden said.

His friends just stared.

Truthfully, it had been Malcolm who'd insisted they send for Raff and Benedict. He'd seemed to think they might know how best to handle this new turn of events. But by the looks of it, they were just as rattled by it all as he and Malcolm were.

"What were you thinking when you climbed up there?" Benedict finally asked.

Hayden shrugged.

"He'd been drinking," Malcolm said by way of explanation.

"Ah, of course." Raff crossed his arms, looking every bit the arrogant duke. "So, you went up there without a plan and—"

"I didn't think I'd need a plan," he said. "I honestly didn't really believe she'd be there. I mean, a maid in a tower?" He shook his head, eyes wide as he threw his hands out. "It sounded like fiction."

"And yet you went up there anyway," Benedict pointed out.

Malcolm's voice was droll. "He called it his quest. One last grand adventure before he chose his bride or some such nonsense."

Hayden was too used to his friends' mockery to be overly irritated now. And besides, they were right to mock him. It had been a foolish whim. An imbecilic dare that had been brought on by his own big mouth at the gaming hell.

"The good news is," Malcolm continued. "You undoubtedly won the wager."

Hayden grunted in rueful amusement. "Wonderful."

"I certainly hope you won a fortune in exchange for marrying some woman you don't even know," Raff said.

"Was she really a prisoner up there?" Benedict asked. His voice had always been low, but ever since the fire that had left scars all across his neck and the left side of his face, his voice had a raspy quality to it that made him sound more grim than ever.

Hayden nodded. He couldn't bring himself to make a glib remark on that front. He wasn't sure he'd ever forget the sight he'd first beheld. The girl was frighteningly frail. All skin and bones before she'd covered herself. And there'd been bruises along with those dark circles under her eyes and the even darker emotions in her gaze.

He'd seen more fear and courage in the eyes of that dark-haired slip of a lady than he'd ever seen in his whole life.

"What for?" Raff asked, his brows drawn together in confusion. "Was she born on the wrong side of the blanket?"

Hayden shrugged.

Raff arched a brow, his eyes sharp and alert. "Do you not know, or do you not care?"

"Both," he shot back. "It makes no difference. I'm marrying her either way."

That had all three of his friends staring at him again.

He scrubbed a hand over his gritty eyes. "Can we talk about this in the morning? I'm ready to keel over at the moment."

"Stay here tonight," Malcolm said. "We'll ready a room so you don't have to go home. The girl is in a stranger's house. She might feel better knowing her fiancé is here as well."

He let out a humorless chuckle. "You seem to forget that I'm a stranger to her just as much as you are."

"Yes," Benedict said slowly. "But you're the stranger she's to marry." His gaze was narrowed and dark. "Do not take that lightly, old friend. She's placing her safety and her very life in your hands for the keeping."

Hayden opened his mouth, ready to retort with a quip—but it withered and died on his tongue.

A heavy weight settled on his chest, and he found himself absently rubbing his ribcage as he tried to take in the enormity of what he'd done.

She was his now. His to take care of.

He waited for panic to set in. After all, he'd put off marriage all these years for a reason. He loved his freedom, and he'd never met a woman he could trust enough that he'd give that up for her. Besides, his father had hardly set a good example with the women he'd chosen.

But the panic never came. If anything, he just felt…tired. Tired but resolved and content and…

Maybe even a little excited about what was to come next.

"You two can stay here tonight as well, if you'd like," Malcolm was saying to the others. "I do hate that we dragged you over here so late."

"As if we'd miss this news," Raff chuckled.

Hayden leaned forward. "Actually, there was another reason we wanted you here."

Malcolm nodded. "That's right. We need to acquire a special license for our friend here." He looked to Hayden who nodded. They'd briefly discussed this before Raff and Benedict had arrived.

"I need a special license, but with a minimum of questions. Or explanations." He winced. "Not for my sake, you know, but…" His gaze slid toward the doorway and the staircase beyond where he'd last seen Madeline disappear.

"Of course," Raff said. "The sooner you marry her the better."

Benedict scowled. "We'll have to discuss what story to tell."

He meant in society. How to account for this new lady, who would now be a marchioness. How to excuse her absence all these years. And how to explain their meeting.

Benedict, Raff, and Malcolm all looked to him.

"Tomorrow," he said. "That's a matter we ought to discuss with the lady herself, and she needs her rest. We all do."

Everyone agreed to this.

"Will you stay?" Malcolm asked.

"I shouldn't," Raff said. "Evangeline will be worried if I'm gone too long."

"Yes, and Philippa will be beside herself waiting to hear the latest news."

They all exchanged a knowing look.

Malcolm spoke first. "Something tells me Hayden's fiancée is going to have several visitors tomorrow."

Hayden's fiancée. Something shifted and settled at the sound of it. His shoulders went back and his spine straightened. This new responsibility didn't feel like the dreaded weight he'd thought it would be.

More like…an honor. His purpose.

"Good," he said when he realized the others were watching him. "I don't know much about her life in that home, but I'm certain she could use friends."

"In that case," Raff said. "We shall bring our wives when we come to call tomorrow."

He and Benedict exchanged a look.

"After we've called on the archbishop about that license," Benedict added.

"Good, good." Hayden nodded, his head starting to throb now that the last of the alcohol had left his system.

Vivian arrived in the hallway just as Benedict and Raff were taking their leave.

"Madeline, is she..." Hayden started and stopped. "Is she well?"

Vivian's smile was rueful. "As well as can be expected. She did not say much to me or her maid, aside from expressing her gratitude."

"She's in her bedroom now," she said, her gaze on Hayden.

"May I..." His throat felt too dry, his chest too tight. "May I see her before...before I retire?"

Her lips twitched, and all three of his friends were staring at him like they'd never seen him before. "Certainly. I'll go with you and make sure she's still awake."

And if she wishes to see you.

That much was left unspoken. Vivian really was too kind. Nerves made him restless and tense as they left the others, and he slipped into the library and snagged a book of poetry so he wouldn't be empty-handed when he saw her.

When they approached Madeline's closed door, Vivian knocked and then slipped inside, closing the door behind her.

A moment later, she reappeared.

Hayden hadn't realized he'd been holding his breath until Vivian smiled and told him to go on in.

"I won't keep her long," he murmured as he passed.

He walked in slowly, afraid of startling her, but she was sitting upright in bed and staring over at him.

He smiled, hoping it would put her at ease. Then he walked over to the side of the bed and sank down beside her.

She didn't shrink away from him, but she didn't return his smile either.

Time. It would take time, that was all. She'd have to learn how to trust him, just as he trusted her.

The thought knocked him upside the head. Did he trust her? He supposed he had no reason to, but even less reason not to. After all, he'd been the one to get her into this situation. She hadn't trapped him.

"Do you have everything you need?" he asked.

"Yes." Her voice was little more than a whisper. "Lady Fallenmore was most generous."

She looked down at the silk wrap that covered her in place of that pale, tattered cotton rag she'd been wearing.

His palms were clammy as he tried to find words to soothe her. His grip tightened on the book in his hands as he held it out to her. "I thought perhaps…" He cleared his throat. "When I'm troubled, I find reading calms the mind."

Truthfully, it was whiskey that typically calmed his mind, but he'd heard reading was a good distraction as well.

Her eyes widened a bit, and her lips parted. She took the book from his hands. "Thank you," she whispered.

Another silence fell between them.

"Madeline, I just wanted to say…" He stopped.

What?

Sorry for falling through your window?

Thank you for coming away with me?

He cleared his throat. "I just wanted to say goodnight."

She smiled, and he felt his insides tilt before repositioning themselves.

She truly was beautiful. Too thin, perhaps, and her cheeks were too hollow. But she had wide, dark eyes, delicate features, and thick dark curls that were now damp and loose around her shoulders.

She was gorgeous, and…and she was his.

The thought was so very humbling, he couldn't bring himself to be charming or clever.

But the silence was stretching too long, and she looked like she might fall over with exhaustion. He reached out slowly, pausing when she flinched. He let his hand drop on top of hers and smoothed a thumb over the back of her hand, feeling an awareness stir at that slight contact.

This woman would be his wife.

He swallowed thickly. "Get some rest," he said, forcing himself to move away. To get far away from her before he gave into temptation and kissed those lush lips. "We'll have much to discuss in the morning, but for now, please know that you are safe and…cared for."

Her brows arched slightly in surprise.

Truthfully, he'd surprised himself.

"I'll be near if you need anything," he said.

She lifted a hand. "Goodnight, my lord."

"Hayden," he corrected. "And goodnight."

Chapter Five

MADELINE HAD NO idea what to make of it all.

She'd been in this house for nearly a day. For hours she'd sat here with these kind, welcoming ladies, and she still wasn't sure what they expected of her.

But, as she sat on the settee in Lord and Lady Fallenmore's drawing room, it was clear that something was expected of her.

"Perhaps you'd like some more tea," Lady Raffian said.

No, *Evangeline*. The beautiful blonde kept insisting that Madeline call her Evangeline.

"No, thank you," Madeline said.

Evangeline looked to the woman with auburn hair and a dazzling smile to her left—a countess just like Madeline's mother. Lady Foster, but she insisted that Madeline call her Philippa.

"I do hope you know you can trust us, dear," Philippa said, reaching across the table cluttered with teacups to pat Madeline's hand. "We've all been where you are, and there are no three women who could better understand if you have any questions or…reservations about your upcoming marriage."

Reservations? Madeline glanced over at the other redhead, her hostess Lady Fallenmore.

No, *Vivian*.

Lud, but this did not come easily to her. They honestly expected Madeline to use their given names as if they were her dearest friends.

"I appreciate that, Lady…er, Philippa. But I have no questions," she said.

In fact, she had many questions. But none that these women could answer for her.

She couldn't bring herself to say she had no reservations. That was too big of a lie. She was filled with nothing but reservations.

Exhaustion had claimed her easily enough last night, but whatever fears and second thoughts she'd avoided the evening before hit her smack in the face the moment she rose.

A clock ticked in the corner, and Vivian gave her another gentle smile. While she had red hair like Philippa, Vivian seemed a little older and had a more maternal air about her, while Philippa seemed to spark with energy beside sweet, quiet Evangeline.

"Are you…are you all right with the fact that you're marrying Hayden?" Philippa asked, the words bursting forth as if she couldn't hold them back for one more moment.

The other two cast Philippa wide-eyed looks, and Madeline had to bite back a smile at Philippa's look of chagrin.

But then all eyes were on her again as they awaited an answer.

And how to answer such a question?

Was she all right?

Does it matter? She wanted to shoot back.

"I…" She cleared her throat. "I know it is necessary. And I am fortunate…in many ways."

This was all true. Thanks to her mother and Mr. Foley's little event where she was on display as some sort of sacrifice—or worse, some possession to be bought and used—she was now all too aware of what fate had in store for her before Hayden came along.

And as far as future husbands go, he seemed nice enough.

A smile tugged at her lips at the memory of him holding a

book out to her. He'd looked so sincere and hopeful.

She hadn't had the heart to tell him she did not know how to read.

Her smile fell flat as shame filled her chest and made her hands tighten into fists. She ought to know her letters, at the very least.

This kind, titled gentleman was going to make her his wife, and she couldn't even read.

He could likely have any lady he wanted as a wife, and he'd be stuck with her. Uneducated and unpolished. She didn't know the first thing about being a wife, let alone a marchioness.

No one could deny he was also handsome.

But a charming smile and kind eyes were hardly a true indication of a man's character, now were they?

He drank, she knew that. What if he was a mean drunk? Or what if he grew violent like her father and beat her, or…

Or what?

She'd be no worse off than she had been before.

Still, she supposed there was something to be said for familiarity, even when it was awful. There was an odd sort of comfort in knowing one's doom. But surely the life Hayden offered would be better than anything she could expect with any of those leering, grasping men.

The three ladies were still watching her expectantly.

"Is he…" She wet her lips, her voice cracking under the weight of their stares. "Is Hayden coming back?"

"Oh yes, of course," Vivian said quickly.

He'd been gone by the time Madeline had mustered the courage to leave her room. Some part of her was afraid she'd get in trouble for leaving her quarters without being fetched, but Vivian had greeted her warmly as she'd explained that she'd just missed Hayden.

"He and the other men should be back soon enough," Vivian continued. "Once they obtain the special license."

Madeline nodded, her hands twisting in her lap. The special

license.

To marry.

Panic reared up sudden and unexpected. Her heart raced like mad at the enormity of what she was about to do.

Oh, good God, she had to get out of here. She had to escape. Her gaze darted around the room, but there were no doors in here, only the one leading out into the hallway.

And where would she go?

She forced herself to take a deep, calming breath. This urge to run, it was merely fear at work. She had to stop. Had to think.

"Madeline, I..." Evangeline blushed. "I did not wish to marry Raff."

Madeline stilled. The others turned to Evangeline with sympathetic expressions.

"It was a very difficult time for me. And obviously, Raff and I, we...we worked it out. We are quite happily in love now," she added with a grin. "But I know I would have given anything to have had a friend in my corner. Someone to talk to."

Vivian took over. "I think what Evangeline is saying is that even though you might not know us well—"

"Yet," Philippa interjected.

"Even though you don't know us well *yet*," Vivian amended with a smile. "We should very much like to be friends with you. And we hope that you will come to any one of us if you need to talk or if you have any questions..."

Madeline cast another look at the other ladies as her brows drew together in confusion.

There was that mention of questions again. What did they think she had questions about?

It was Philippa who stopped treading lightly around the topic. She leaned forward with a sigh. "Madeline, dearest, do you know what a man expects of a woman when they're wed?"

Madeline's cheeks caught fire but she nodded quickly. "I think so. At least, I have an idea."

Not much of an idea, but sadly the way those men touched

her. The lewd words she'd overheard and the way they'd looked at her…

She shrank back on the settee now, her breathing coming in shallow gasps.

Was that what Hayden would do to her? Was that what he expected as well?

Another silent exchange occurred between the other women as if they were trying to decide if that answer was good enough.

Fortunately, just then the doors to the drawing room opened and the four men appeared. For a moment, all was chaos as the husbands and wives sought each other out, and everyone seemed to be talking over one another.

Hayden cut through the others, and his gaze sought her out. Was it her imagination or did he seem to breathe a sigh of relief to find her sitting there?

Surely it was her imagination. And yet, she couldn't quite help the smile she gave him in turn. It felt like the first genuine smile to grace her lips all day, and she breathed out a sigh of relief of her own.

Though for the life of her, she couldn't explain it.

Maybe it was the fact that he seemed familiar. More familiar, at least, than the others here in this room.

"How are you?" he asked as he sat beside her.

She nodded. *All right. I'm fine.* She couldn't say a word. This close, she could smell his warm scent, and it reminded her of the night before. When he'd come to say goodnight and his very presence had made her feel like she was living in a dream.

No one was this kind to her. No one said goodnight to her with that much affection or smiled at her with that much kindness.

Well, no one aside from Albert, but he didn't make her belly flutter like Hayden did.

Was that normal?

For a moment, she wished she'd asked that of her new lady friends.

"Did you…did you get it?" she asked.

He reached for her hand and squeezed, his smile triumphant. "I did."

"*We* did," Lord Raffian corrected with a laugh.

Lord Fallenmore clapped the large, scarred earl beside him on the back. "I'd say most of the credit goes to our intimidating friend here."

Philippa grinned up at him, unabashedly loving, and his lips quirked at the corners. "I suppose sometimes the beastly appearance can be a boon."

Madeline looked to Hayden, who winked down at her as he covered her hand with his.

"It took a little convincing, especially considering I had to be rather…artful with my excuses."

She blushed as she dipped her head.

The others were all noisily laughing and talking amongst themselves. She felt Hayden's fingers beneath her chin tilting her face up gently. So very gently it made her chest tighten.

When was the last time anyone had ever touched her so gently?

"All will be well, Madeline," he said.

She nodded because it seemed to be what he wanted.

"I'm sorry." The whisper came out of her before she could stop it.

His brows arched. "You're sorry? I'm the dolt who came barging in on you."

"Yes, but…you shouldn't have to be stuck with me."

And stuck he was.

Just as she was trapped. Thoroughly. Completely.

She glanced around frantically. Oh goodness, she needed some air, that was all.

"Would you take a turn about the room with me?" he asked.

She nodded. What else could she do? And soon they were striding away from the others, slowly pacing the lengths of the room. To what end? They were going in circles.

"Is this…" She glanced up hesitantly. "Is this something that courting couples do?"

His lips wobbled like he was fighting a smile. "I've heard they do, but I'll admit, I'm not quite certain what the point of it is."

A laugh slipped out of her mouth, startling her. She couldn't recall the last time she'd heard her own laughter. "I suppose it gives a couple some privacy."

"Mmm." He glanced over meaningfully to where the other three couples were all watching them, not even trying to pretend they weren't. "Not much privacy though, eh?"

"No," she agreed.

They fell silent again, and she grew painfully aware of him. All of him. All six-feet-whatever he was. He was tall and he was broad…

But he didn't use that to intimidate her.

And yet, she was still a little intimidated.

"One day, I hope you'll speak to me about what your life was like growing up in that household," he said slowly. "I will not push you to tell me. But from what I saw, well…" He turned and cupped her face between his hands, his expression unnervingly earnest. "I want you to know that I will take care of you now. You are safe with me. Do you understand?"

She nodded, her breath hitching in her lungs. He seemed so sincere. And yet…

The way he was holding her face, the odd intensity in his eyes—it made her heart lurch with fear. She knew well the sort of lunacy that heightened emotions could lead to, and she backed away from him with a pounding heart.

He let her go, watching her steadily. "Did I do something wrong?"

She shook her head, swallowing hard.

He looked like he might ask more questions, but then his demeanor changed, and he smiled once more. "Madeline, I brought someone here to see you."

She glanced around in question.

"A surgeon," he continued. "He's trustworthy, and well respected, though he's not one that members of the *ton* would call for. It didn't seem prudent to set tongues wagging before the wedding was announced."

She frowned. "A surgeon? What for?"

"Just to check you over, to make sure you are well—"

"I am not sick," she said. Her heart tripped and fell. A surgeon. She'd heard her father ranting about doctors enough to know that they could hurt you.

They could touch you and give you drugs.

She backed away further. "I don't want some strange man touching me."

"You have nothing to fear, Madeline. I could go with you if you'd like. Make sure no one harms you." She winced at the thought of two men alone with her. He glanced over to Vivian, who was watching them closely. "Or I could have Vivian go with you. She will ensure your safety."

It seemed as if everyone in the room was watching her now, and her legs began to tremble.

He offered his arm. "I promise you, Madeline. I will not let anyone hurt you ever again."

A short time later, she was alone in a room with the surgeon, Doctor Sinclair. Though Vivian had indeed offered to accompany her, in the end, Madeline opted to see him alone.

He seemed older than Hayden, but not by much, and his sandy-blonde hair fell to his shoulders. He put her at ease quickly with his calm voice and gentle hands.

He did not force her to disrobe, and his brief inspection was done before she knew it.

"You need to eat," he said. "You are malnourished and it shows. I suspect there are other injuries as well. Injuries I cannot see…"

She stared back at him blankly. She was not stupid. She knew what he meant, but she had no desire to speak with him about her life before this moment, nor of the events the night Hayden had stolen her away.

He was right though. There were no bruises where those men had touched her, but she still felt their fingers and smelled their rancid breath like the moment had been imprinted in her memory.

He crossed his arms and regarded her with a sigh. "How much do you know about doctors, Lady Madeline?"

She blinked at the title. She supposed technically she was an earl's daughter, but no one had ever called her lady before. In her household, even the servants knew that she was the bastard girl. The prisoner in the tower. She was anything but a lady.

Madeline shook her head when she realized he was waiting for an answer. How much did she know? Blessedly little.

"Part of this profession includes acting as a confidante. I cannot discuss your health with others. Anything you say to me as a patient stays strictly between us."

Her brows hitched up. "Truly?"

He nodded and watched her. "I do not know how you came to be here or why you look as though you've suffered at the hands of others. But you must know that if you need me, I am here to help you. I owe no allegiance to your fiancé or his friends. My sole duty as your physician is to you and you alone."

Her lips parted. So much kindness in one day from so many strangers.

"I don't believe you could help me," she said slowly. "I am…that is…Hayden and I are both caught in a situation, you see…"

He nodded as if he did see.

He couldn't possibly.

"Is there anyone who can help you?" He seemed to be choosing his words cautiously. "A message to relay, perhaps?"

He'd gotten it all wrong. She could see it in his eyes. He was angry with Hayden and the others. He thought they were doing wrong by her. But that wasn't the case at all.

And yet…

And yet, she didn't know the man she was to wed. What if all these smiles and his kindness were just a ruse for the others? What if she got to know him and despised him? She recalled that flash of intensity in his eyes. Possessiveness and need and—

She shuddered. And that dark desire she'd seen in the eyes of those men who'd touched her so horribly.

She shook her head, swallowing down bile.

The doctor was waiting for some sort of response. She wet her lips to say "no, there's nothing you can do" but then her mind caught on the phrase he'd used—a message to relay.

She straightened. A surge of hope flaring. It wasn't exactly an escape from all this, but it would be her saving grace if Hayden wasn't the man he seemed.

"Could you…could you write a note for me?" she asked. "I do not know my letters and—"

"Yes. Of course." He sought out the materials without a single question and wrote her message with a furrowed brow.

"I've been forced to marry," she said softly, watching the doctor's hands as he wrote the words. "Please help me…"

True concern was in his eyes when he finished and read over what he'd written and held it up for her perusal. As the letters blurred in a meaningless patter, all she could do was nod and trust that he'd written what she'd said.

"Shall I post it for you? Whom may I address it to?"

She wet her lips and shook her head. That was the trouble. She didn't know where Albert was or how to find him. "I will handle that if need be."

If need be.

If Hayden turned out to be a monster, well…at least this time she wouldn't be trapped without some sort of escape in place.

Not again.

Never again.

CHAPTER SIX

THE MINUTES BEFORE Hayden's wedding crawled by.

Hayden thrust a hand through his hair and eyed the bottle of whiskey on Malcolm's end table in his study.

"Do not even think it," Benedict growled.

Hayden sighed. "I won't do it. I know I need my wits about me today more than ever."

"An odd thing to say on one's wedding day," Raff chuckled. "Sounds like you're about to enter a business negotiation."

Hayden scoffed. "That part's done, thank God."

"How'd it go?" Malcolm asked.

Hayden shook his head, the rage he'd felt the other morning when he'd faced the countess back in full force. "She's ruthless, that one."

"Was the mad earl there as well?" Raff sounded curious. "I've never even seen the old coot."

"Neither have I," Hayden admitted. "He didn't show. Only the countess and that snake Foley."

Benedict growled. "What's he doing hovering around that decrepit old manor?"

"Whatever it is, he's up to no good," Malcolm said.

Raff glowered. "I should have killed him when I had the chance."

Hayden scrubbed a hand over his face. He didn't even want

to think about the meeting with the countess or her smug right-hand man.

"But what's he about?" Benedict demanded. "He must have some stake in this. We ought to be prepared."

Raff shook his head. "The man is desperate for power. It doesn't surprise me one bit that he'd attach himself to a corrupt countess."

"No doubt they have a common goal," Malcolm agreed.

Hayden grunted his agreement. "They do, all right. They're both hungry for a fortune, and they'll do just about anything to get it."

"I take it no dowry then," Malcolm said.

Hayden shook his head. "No. But you know I don't care about that." His father had been a nasty old bugger, but he'd had a head for numbers and the marquessate was flush with coin. "The countess outright asked me for a large sum in exchange for her approval of this marriage."

The others stared at him wide-eyed.

"She didn't," Malcolm said.

"What did you say?" Benedict asked.

"I negotiated. For my bride. She made comments about how I was taking away her best chance for a fortune, and so I owed it to her." He added the last part through gritted teeth. Because what he couldn't stand, but what he couldn't stop wondering was—"What had she planned for Madeline if I hadn't come along?"

The other three shared wary looks. It seemed no one wanted to hedge a guess.

"But you still gave her the money?" Benedict looked affronted by this.

"Not everything she asked for. She'd overreached, and we all knew it. I agreed to fund some much-needed renovations on their property and have my man advise her son on ways they could shore up their funds."

Raff scowled. "Where *is* the son?"

Hayden's jaw tightened as well. That had been his question, too. The father was clearly ill, mentally and physically, judging by his absence. But what was the son's excuse? "He's off managing estates in the south, she said."

"Does he know how she'd been mistreating his sister?" Malcolm asked.

"Had he known all this time and done nothing?" Benedict added.

Hayden had no answer. He didn't even know the full extent of what his wife-to-be had experienced in that household. But anyone could see it had not been good.

It rather put his own miserable childhood in perspective.

He eyed the whiskey again, but the twinge of longing to drown his own memories wasn't as strong as his desire to ensure this day went smoothly for Madeline.

She was likely scared. And who could blame her? He'd visited her every day this week, and they'd gotten on well enough with pleasant if one-sided conversations. He'd done most of the talking, filling her in on his estates and what she could expect when she came to live with him.

He tried to assess her interests and hobbies, but she was tight-lipped about herself and her past. She had no knowledge of current fashions and had gone along with Vivian's plan of purchasing her some simple ready-to-wear gowns from a local shop until the seamstress could make her custom collection.

But again, Madeline hadn't had much of an opinion on any of it. She was polite to a fault with him and the others, but he couldn't ignore this feeling that she was hiding in plain sight. Trying her best to please and not cause any trouble.

The thought made him frown. He wanted her to be comfortable. With him and with his friends. But how?

A knock on the study door had all of them straightening.

Vivian poked her head in with a smile.

"Is it time?" Hayden asked. His insides leapt with excitement more than nerves. Which was...alarming. But not bad, he supposed.

This whole situation would be much worse if he was dreading his own wedding. And he wasn't. His blood ran hot at the mere thought of his bride. She looked healthier with each new visit, and as she'd warmed up to him with sweet smiles, he'd found himself looking forward to those moments when he could steal her away. Have her all to himself.

She was beautiful, he'd always known that, but it was more than that. It was the warmth and intelligence in her eyes, the way she listened so thoughtfully and moved with such grace.

"It's not quite time," Vivian said. "But your fiancée would like a word alone with you before the wedding."

"Oh." He shot up out of his seat, his heart lurching as well. "Of course. Yes, of course."

He didn't miss his friends' grins. As if any of them had been any more composed on their own wedding days.

He followed Vivian out and up the stairs to Madeline's room.

"Is she…" *Oh, blast.* He cleared his throat. "She's not having second thoughts, is she?"

Vivian's gaze held more than a little sympathy. "I don't believe so. But she is understandably nervous."

He nodded. "Of course, of course."

And for some reason, learning about her nerves helped to ease his own. He would soothe her and take care of her.

The thought had him picking up his pace, eager to be at her side.

How odd. All these years of avoiding a responsibility such as this one, and now that it was here—he rather liked it.

No, not just liked it. It gave him a sense of purpose that he'd never had before. No one had ever needed him before, and the weight of that responsibility didn't weigh on him like an anchor the way he'd expected it to. If anything, it was a pleasant weight that made him feel grounded and settled.

Vivian tapped on the door lightly before letting him in. She smiled at Hayden. "I don't suppose I need to chaperone you two since you'll be man and wife any moment now."

He returned her smile, but one glance at Madeline's rigid form and he said softly, "Let's leave the door open, all the same."

Vivian nodded and spoke a little louder for Madeline's sake. "I'll be just outside the door if you need me."

Madeline sat utterly still on the edge of her bed.

She was so still…and so bloody gorgeous that it took Hayden a full moment before he could speak. "You look beautiful, Madeline."

Madeline blushed and dipped her head.

He approached and sat beside her. "You wished to talk to me?"

When she looked up, her expression was pained. "I wanted to be sure that you knew…before today. Before…"

Before they wed.

"That I knew what, love?" He tensed, unsure what he was dreading.

"That I am not legitimate," she said.

He let out a rush of air.

"My father claimed me and my mother, er, the countess claimed to be my mother, but…"

"It's all right, love," he said. "I figured as much."

"You did?"

"No mother would treat her own daughter the way the countess treated you."

He tasted the lie in his words. His father had been cruel to him, and his own mother had abandoned him, but…

But he'd known the moment he'd met the countess that she'd hated Madeline in a way no woman could despise her own flesh and blood. It was clear in the countess's every look, word, and gesture.

"And you…you would still marry me?" she asked.

He touched her chin, bringing her gaze up to meet his. "I made my choice, love. I made it the moment I foolishly decided to climb a tower and prove that you did not exist—"

This earned him a wobbly smile.

"And I made that choice again when I told your mother I was making you my bride." He took a deep breath. "This is not to say there will not be challenges in store for you when we leave the safety of this house. You will be gossiped about and judged, I dare say." He frowned at the thought of it. "I wish I could protect you from every vicious rumor and all the spiteful gossip, Madeline, but—"

She kissed him. The soft but sudden touch of her lips to his cut him off mid-sentence.

He froze. Or rather, every inch of him flooded with heat, but he forced himself to remain still as her warm, soft lips pressed against his. She did not open them or move them in any way.

It was the untutored kiss of a naive girl, and somehow that made it all the more sweet.

His ribcage tightened, his chest aching horribly at the innocence in that kiss. The trust.

That above all had him holding still despite the fact that his hands clenched and his arms shook with the need to pull her into his arms.

But he had this feeling—a knowing, really—that it would only push her away.

She pulled back after a heartbeat, the kiss lasting no more than a second, her cheeks flushed and her eyes wide. "I'm sorry, I…I thought…I wanted to see…"

"Don't apologize." Ah hell, his voice sounded much too gruff. He reached up to touch her cheek. "Never apologize." He tried to lighten his tone. "Definitely not for kissing me."

Her answering smile was shy but dubious. "Did I do it right?"

And there went his heart, twisting and writhing as it gave up the fight. "It was perfect," he said. "And you are welcome to kiss me whenever you wish. Wherever you wish." He paused. "For however long you wish."

That did it. She burst out in a giggle that made his heart slam furiously. He couldn't have stopped his own answering grin if he'd tried.

"All right then," she said.

He leaned over and pressed a gentle kiss to her forehead. "All right then."

"Shall I…er…" She pursed her lips, her brows drawn together. "I've never done anything like this before, shall I…do I go first?"

He chuckled, wrapping an arm around her shoulders to give her a quick squeeze. "Truthfully, I've never been married before either. Let's go down there together, shall we?"

She smiled as she nodded, taking his arm when they stood. As he led her down, he couldn't help but marvel at his good fortune.

To think, all these years he'd avoided matrimony like the plague, so certain he'd never find a woman he could trust. Never thinking he'd find someone sincere, who looked beyond his title and his fortune.

But now here she was. A woman so pure and guileless it tugged at his heart every time he looked upon her. The way she looked at him like he was indeed the hero of the tale, the way she trusted him to take care of her.

He placed his hand over hers as they met up with the others in the parlor where the intimate wedding was to be held.

And he *would* take care of her. A possessiveness the likes of which he'd never known caught him in its grip and made him feel like another man entirely.

A new man.

A man with a purpose.

And as he gazed down into Madeline's sweet face, he knew that purpose was her. To protect her. To make her happy.

And to destroy anyone or anything that threatened to harm her.

CHAPTER SEVEN

HAYDEN'S HOME WAS lovely.

Too lovely, in fact, if such a thing was possible.

Madeline toyed with the knife beside her plate, too nervous to eat the dinner his staff had prepared. The dining room was so very large. The silverware was so polished and the furniture ornate…

Nerves made Madeline's belly swarm.

The servants were very deferential, almost as if…

Almost as if you are their marchioness?

She reached for a glass of water.

You are the marchioness, you ninny. And she'd better get used to it.

"Will you give us a moment, please?" Hayden's voice from the far end of the candlelit table startled her. For a moment, she thought he was talking to her. But he was addressing the footmen who were hovering nearby. They filed out, leaving her alone with Hayden.

Hayden stood and strode toward her, stopping at the seat beside hers. He pulled it out and sat. "There, that's better." He reached for her hand. "Now, what can I do to put you at ease?"

She smiled, ready to deny that she was uneasy, but how could she? "I…I don't know. I'm sorry. I've just…I've never even seen a place so grand."

"You grew up in a grand home yourself." His eyes were kind, but there were questions there she didn't want to face.

She didn't want to talk about her childhood or how he'd come to find her. She'd always known it was unusual. Even without Albert's guidance, she would have figured that out. But he'd made sure to teach her what life was like outside their estate walls as a child. And with his stories, he'd given her glimpses of the outside world when she'd matured into a young lady and her father had locked her away.

For her own safekeeping, her father had said.

Her father was prone to paranoia, as well as fits of rage. When he wasn't punishing her for some made-up misdeeds, he was protecting her virtue under lock and key.

No, not normal.

Indeed, Albert had long since convinced her that their father was just as mad as his enemies suggested.

"Our house might have been grand once," she said. "But my father had sold off most of the furniture and paintings when I was a girl. And the countess sold off the rest these last few years since…well, since she took control."

He nodded. "Well, then," he said in a more cheerful tone. "Would it make you feel better if I told the servants to hide the fine furnishings and paintings?"

She laughed at his teasing. "No, my lord."

"Hayden," he chided gently. "Or William, if you prefer. Though no one's called me that since my mother left."

"When was that?"

He looked away. "I was ten when she left us for another. She died shortly after that." His gaze darted back to her. "That's not public knowledge."

She smiled. "Who would I tell?"

He returned her smile. "My father remarried."

"Did you get on well with your stepmother?"

"No."

She blinked at his tone, but the coldness was there and gone by the time he spoke again a second later.

"But she's gone, as well, so there's no need to talk about her."

"Did she pass away as well?"

"No. I sent her away."

"I see." Her belly tightened at the flare of anger she caught in his eyes. She'd gotten so used to seeing nothing but warmth and kindness, anything else seemed unnerving.

He glanced down at her plate. "You've barely eaten a thing." He arched his brows. "That won't do at all."

Her lips parted in surprise when he plucked a berry from the bowl of fruit beside her plate. He held it up to her mouth, his thumb grazing her lower lip, which sent a shock of sensations through her. Suddenly she was very, very aware of how close he was.

She also couldn't stop thinking about how it had felt to touch her lips to his.

It had been a quick, and quite possibly foolish act, but it had felt necessary at the time. She'd been so afraid—well, she was still a little afraid—of what it would be like when he touched her...intimately.

She couldn't imagine his touch without stirring up memories of those vile men. And she had to be certain...

She couldn't have married him if his touch made her feel so wretched, if a mere kiss made her want to be sick.

In that particular moment, it had seemed a good idea. Like perhaps if she took control, she could overcome her fear.

It had worked...to some extent. The touch of his lips to hers hadn't been the same at all. But it had led to a shocking sensation that left her skin feeling raw and sensitive, while her belly had dipped low.

And now that sensation was back as his thumb brushed her lip and his dark gaze met hers. There was no laughter but no anger either. He looked at her like she was the only person in the world, and Madeline wondered if this was what men felt like when they imbibed.

Surely it was something like this because it made her head swim.

"Go on," he urged, his voice husky.

She parted her mouth further, and when he pressed the berry between his lips, she gasped at the brief touch of his skin to her tongue. It was an effort to swallow. But he was back soon enough with another berry. "It's my job now," he said, "to make sure you are fed and content."

She smiled this time as she let him feed her. And when her tongue touched his thumb, she didn't jerk away. Twice more he fed her, and then his gaze dipped to her lips. "How are they?"

She didn't exactly mean to moan, but there was something intoxicating about the intimacy. For a girl who was rarely touched in anything other than anger, his gentleness was…well, *delicious*.

He leaned in closer, his gaze dipping to her lips. "May I have a taste?"

Her breath caught, and something odd happened between her thighs. Heat was building, uncomfortable and embarrassing. "Y-yes."

He did exactly as he'd said. He tasted her. He caught her lower lip between his and sucked gently.

She couldn't breathe. Couldn't think. Was this…

Was this kissing?

He tipped his head slightly, until he was gliding his lips over the corner of her mouth. Then his tongue flicked out, and he tasted her upper lip. Her eyelids fluttered closed at the sweet assault. Her breath was shaky.

"You taste delicious," he murmured when he moved his mouth to her ear. His breath there made her shiver. But she wasn't cold.

Oh no, she wasn't the least bit cold. If anything, she felt as though she'd caught fire. Her veins seemed to sing with this newfound pleasure, and that heat between her thighs had turned to a throbbing ache.

"Let me take care of you upstairs," he said, reaching for her hand. "Let me show you pleasure."

She went with him willingly. For a little while, she even forgot to be nervous. He wanted to bed her. She understood this. But it didn't feel so terrifying when her heart was fluttering so wildly and his every touch was so gentle and warm.

He led her into her room. The room she'd been shown to only earlier today. Her new lady's maid had already unpacked her few belongings, and she hadn't dallied long. Once again, the sight of the opulence threw her.

She stopped short just inside the door, and her hand fell from his as he continued inside.

He turned with an expression of concern. "Are you all right?"

"Yes, just…" She swallowed hard. The room was well lit, with a fire roaring in the fireplace and wine set out on an end table. "It's all just so new."

"Of course." He sounded serious. "I should have realized."

He went to her and ran his hands over her shoulders, her arms. "This all must be quite the transition."

She nodded. It was. It most definitely was.

"You've been very brave throughout all of this, Madeline." He leaned forward and kissed her nose, and the innocent gesture made her smile despite her nerves. "I am in awe of your courage."

She blinked, searching his gaze to see if he was mocking her in some way.

He was not.

"I am not brave," she said. "I wish I were."

I might have been. If I'd run away. But instead, you came along and saved me.

"You are." He was gripping her shoulders, his gaze intense. "You have survived the wicked cruelty of others. Being a survivor is courageous, Madeline."

Something in his intensity. Something about the way he said it…

He understood. Maybe not all of it, but he understood.

His thumb brushed over her cheek. "Did they hurt you, love?"

She blinked up at him. Did they hurt her? Her family? Her lips parted, and for a moment she did not know how to answer. "They did not beat me if that is what you mean." They had treated her horribly, but the abuse was not physical. She winced at the memory of her stepmother's cold, hard slaps. Not usually, at least.

Her heart felt heavy in her chest, and for the first time in the week since she'd escaped that tower, she felt an urge to talk. To tell this man every injustice done to her.

"You survived," he continued. "But you don't have to merely survive anymore, Madeline. You are my wife now. You are a marchioness. You have power and wealth and influence—"

She made a choking sound of disbelief, and he stopped with a smile.

"Well. Maybe I cannot make you see that today. Your new life has only just begun. But this is the start, Madeline. Today we start anew. Both of us."

She searched his gaze. He was trying to tell her something. "You wish to start anew as well?"

His smile suddenly struck her as tired and weary. "You'll likely hear stories about me when we make your debut in society. So, you ought to hear it from me first, I suppose."

She tensed.

"I've been a bit of a wastrel these last, oh…ten years or so." His huff of amusement was rueful.

"How?" she asked.

"I have a well-earned reputation for drinking and gambling, and…" He winced. "Reckless acts."

She couldn't stifle a giggle. "Do you mean, for example…climbing up crumbling old tower walls?"

He grinned. "That's one example, yes."

"Is there anything else…" She wet her lips. "Anything I

should know about?"

His brows drew down in confusion.

She swallowed thickly. "I, er, I know what it is to be the illegitimate child of a—"

"No! Oh Christ, no," he said quickly, clearly horrified by the question.

"Sorry, it's just—"

"No, no," he added hurriedly. "You have every right to ask. But the answer is no. I have no children outside of marriage. And I've never been married before so…no. None."

She nodded. "All right."

He smiled. "All right."

The sudden silence terrified her. She forgot to be nervous when he was talking to her and making her laugh. But moments like these, when she realized she had no idea what to say, what to do…

Her eyes widened.

He tugged her forward so she was in his arms. "It's all right, love," he whispered against her ear. "I promised you pleasure, and pleasure you shall have."

She shivered, even though she wasn't quite sure what to expect.

But then he was dipping his head, his lips moving gently over the skin of her neck. Her gasp sounded far too loud as a blistering heat swept through her from head to toe.

"That's it," he murmured. "That's my good girl."

Her next shiver left her trembling. *My good girl.* The words ought to make her feel like a child, but they didn't. She just felt…safe. And cared for.

Like she truly was his and that he would take care of her.

She wondered if he had any idea how wonderful that felt. Better than any physical pleasures ever could.

Her hands fumbled for a bit before she rested them on his shoulders. He stiffened for a second before exhaling loudly. "That's it, love. Touch me anywhere you please."

She kept her hands precisely where they were. Where else did he expect her to touch him?

His hands were roaming. Not aggressive and not so firm as to be painful, but his hands were on her waist and then moving up.

She gasped when they brushed against the underside of her breasts.

His mouth moved to her lips, stealing the gasps as his hands continued the exploration, over her back and up to the exposed skin of her shoulders.

"I want to touch you everywhere," he murmured. "I want to kiss you all over."

She tensed. She squeezed her eyes shut, but it was too late. Images assaulted her. Their faces, their smirks, the dark dangerous lust in their eyes.

Go on. Show us what she's got.

That was what the man with the oily beard had said.

I wouldn't buy a horse without checking its teeth, now would I?

The others had laughed.

Foley had laughed.

The countess had smiled.

Now fingers were tugging at her bodice, seeking out more skin—

"No!" Her voice was shrill and loud.

"Madeline?" Hayden brought his hands up to cup her face. "What is it? Am I moving too quickly?"

She kept her eyes shut, and he muttered an oath.

"Of course, I am."

She felt a blast of cold air when he stepped away from her, letting her go. And all at once, she was freezing, inside and out. Adrift and at sea and—"No. Don't go," she said, opening her eyes wide in panic.

His gaze was so beautifully tender. "Madeline...love. I don't want to scare you."

"I cannot help that I'm scared. But I...I don't want you to go."

A muscle ticked in his jaw as he said gently, "Did your father or your brother…" He cut himself off with an oath. "Did any man in your household ever…touch you."

She blinked in confusion as her mind turned over his words, but her gut coiled in horror as the memory of that night began to play all over again.

Touch her like that, he meant. Had they ever touched her…like that.

He cleared his throat and tried again. "Did anyone ever force you to—"

"No." Her voice was too loud and sharp, and for a moment, she shut her eyes, blocking out the memory. She did not wish to acknowledge it, let alone speak of it. "No man has ever touched me like…like you were just touching me."

She opened her eyes to meet his gaze. It was not a lie, she told herself. No man had ever touched her with such care.

Still, guilt pooled in her belly when she saw the relief in his eyes. It hadn't been a lie…

But it hadn't been the truth either.

The space between them seemed to widen with each passing second, and finally, she reached for him, her hands fluttering nervously against his chest. "Don't leave me."

His expression grew so tender, it made her heart ache. And after a long silence, he nodded, seemingly decided. "You're wary of undressing before me, is that it? You're…shy?"

She nodded. That was part of it.

"I will go to my rooms," he said. "I'll have the maid come and get you changed into more suitable nighttime attire."

Relief was fierce, but on its heels came fears of being abandoned. "But you will…you will come back?"

"Oh love, it's our wedding night," he said with a rueful smile. "I will most definitely be back."

She nodded, her breath too shaky to say much at all.

He left, presumably to call for her lady's maid, and she slumped against the bed, trying to make sense of all that had happened.

She was married.

To a marquess.

She shook her head. How she wished she could talk to Albert. He'd know if she'd been right to leave with Hayden. He'd know if she was putting her trust and faith in the right hands.

She thought so, but…

But what did she know of the world? Of men?

Blessedly little.

She drew out the letter that the physician had drafted for her. It was slightly crumpled. She'd had it in the slim pocket of her gown all day, even during her own wedding. Which seemed a little sacrilegious in an odd sort of way. Making a vow before God while her means of escape sat heavily in her pocket.

She wasn't even sure it would work if it came to that.

It would be something, though. It would be better than being stuck again with no way out.

But for now…

She tucked it into the top drawer of her writing desk. For now, she would hold on to it.

Just in case she was trusting the wrong man.

CHAPTER EIGHT

Hayden had never in his life been more nervous than he was at this very moment. He tapped on the door that connected their rooms, letting himself in when he heard a quiet answer.

He assumed it was assent to come in, but he second-guessed this assumption when he entered to find her curled up in a nightdress, her arms wrapped around her legs, and fear written all over her features.

His heart ached with tenderness.

How to put her at ease?

He had no idea. He'd never bedded a virgin before, and this one was so very sheltered.

She was watching him with wide eyes that made him feel like a predator, so instead of moving directly toward her on the bed, he sat in the armchair beside the fire. "Come," he said, patting his knee. "I promise I will not hurt you."

She bit her lip but slowly uncoiled and did as he bid, approaching him with slow, steady steps until she was just in front of him.

He swallowed hard, his cock stirring at the sight she made. His wife. His bride.

Possessiveness and pride, the need to take care of her—all that mixed with desire and left him gritting his teeth to keep calm.

All he wanted to do was grab her, hold her, and show her just how much he would cherish her.

But her hands were clenched into fists, and she looked terrified.

"Let us make a deal, hmm?" he said as he offered her his hand. When she took it, he tugged gently, and she settled onto his knee.

He just barely bit back a groan. This close, he could smell her feminine scent and feel the softness of her skin. A sweet torturous assault on his senses.

"A deal?" she echoed.

"You tell me what you like and what you do not like. I told you I don't wish to scare you, love, and I meant it."

She nibbled on her lip. "I…I don't want to undress for you."

His brows arched slightly at the fear in her eyes as she said it, but he nodded. He'd not pry. Not tonight. "Very well. May I touch you? On top of your clothing?"

Her eyelids fluttered as she watched his hand on her knee. He was stroking her gently, one arm around her waist.

"Y-yes. That's all right," she whispered.

He nuzzled her ear. "And kisses, love? Are kisses all right?"

She turned her head to face him with a sharp inhale. "Yes."

Her eyes were dark, her pupils large. And he wondered if she had any idea that he could see the hard outline of her nipples where they strained against the fabric.

He leaned in close and claimed the lips she offered. This time she met his kiss with one of her own, her mouth opening for him readily.

"Good girl," he murmured when he pulled back. "You're a quick study, I see."

She blushed and ducked her head.

God, so sweet. Nothing at all like his flirtatious whore of a stepmother or any other lady of his acquaintance, for that matter.

She was almost too good to be true.

He pushed the thought aside. He'd gotten too jaded, he supposed. Too used to everyone around him having an agenda. But not his Madeline.

He cupped her jaw, bringing her back down for another kiss, but this time he let his hands explore. Slowly, gently. And was sure to whisper into her ear, "Just tell me if anything scares you, love."

She nodded, her hands clutching his shoulders as her breasts lifted and fell sharply.

He looked into her eyes, searching out that fear that broke his heart, but all he saw was desire.

Bloody hell. That desire in her eyes was such sweet torment, it took all his control not to lift her up, toss her on the bed, and hitch up her skirt so he could bury himself inside her cunny.

He clenched his jaw tight. Soon. One day soon they'd have that sort of ease in their marriage bed. But she needed to be wooed first. Seduced.

And he would not fail her.

"Does this feel good, love?" he asked as his hand on her knee grew bold, sliding up to her inner thigh and giving the soft flesh a gentle squeeze.

She nodded, her lips parted, and her eyes dazed as she watched his hand.

He dipped his head and moved his lips along the lace edge of her neckline. "And this? Is this all right?"

She shuddered when his movements had her nipples brushing against his chest.

"Y-yes."

He dipped his head lower until his lips grazed over the hard, dark nubs that teased him through the thin fabric. He paused, letting her adjust to the feel of his hot mouth so close to her lovely tits. "And this?" He covered her nipple with his mouth through the fabric, and she whimpered, her hips jerking. He pulled back quickly, gazing up at her lovely face. Was it fear?

But no. There was confusion in her eyes, no fear.

"Did that feel all right?" he asked.

She nodded quickly. "I don't...I don't understand what's happening to me."

"Don't fight it, love," he whispered against the soft curve of her breast. "What's happening is natural. It's your body's way of readying itself for me."

For me. He fought the urge to shout it. *For no one else but me.*

But he didn't have to tell this girl that. He didn't trust the sacred bond of marriage any more than he'd trust a cutpurse alone with an open safe, but this girl?

He trusted her.

Or...he wanted to trust her.

And he needed her to trust him.

"Readying itself for what?" she asked.

Oh, Christ. Alarm shot through him. Was it possible she did not know what happened in the marriage bed?

He grimaced at the memory of her alone in that prison of a bedroom.

Of course, it was possible. Who would have taught her? Her wicked stepmother?

He cleared his throat and loosened his grip on her thigh when he realized he was being too firm. "You see, Madeline, when a man and woman wed, they must...come together to have a baby."

She wiggled her hips, and his hard shaft responded like a hound, sitting up on its hind legs to beg. "Yes, I think..." She wet her lips. "That is, we have animals and...this..."

She shifted, turning to meet his gaze as her movement brought his hard cock right up against the soft mound between her thighs. "This fits here."

He nodded, swallowing convulsively. Not thrusting up against her sex took all of his control.

Her brows drew together. "Will it hurt?"

He winced. "Yes. I'm afraid it will."

She bit her lip, and he leaned forward to kiss it until she released her lip and he sucked it into his mouth, making her moan.

He sat back to meet her gaze. "The first time it will hurt, there is no avoiding that, I'm afraid. But I will do all within my power to ease the pain, and from that point on, I will only ever bring you pleasure in bed, do you understand me?"

He hadn't meant that last part to come out so gruff and harsh, but he was holding onto his control through sheer will, and she nodded quickly, almost eagerly. "Yes, William."

The sound of his given name on her lips made him groan, and he buried a hand in her hair to pull her forward for another kiss. This time she didn't use her hands to hold herself upright and her breasts crushed against his chest.

She moaned again, and the sound sent fire through his veins.

He moved the arm that was around her and gripped her bottom. "Is this all right?"

She nodded eagerly again.

The hand on her thigh moved up slowly. Sweet Jesus, she was so hot. When he slid his fingers between her thighs and cupped her sex through her nightgown, she stilled and he groaned.

Even through the fabric, he could feel how wet she was. The thin cotton was soaked through, and the wet heat against his fingers made his mind go blank with everything but sheer desire.

She pulled her head back, and he caught sight of her flaming cheeks.

"No, love. Do not be embarrassed. Never be embarrassed in front of me."

"I'm…" She swallowed audibly. "I'm sorry, I'm wet down there and—"

He clapped a hand on her buttocks again, harder this time to get her attention. Her eyes flew up to his as her breath caught, and her hips rolled on instinct.

"What did I tell you about apologizing?" he said.

For a moment, he was afraid he'd scared her, but instead, she melted into him, her eyelids lowering slightly like she was hypnotized.

"Good girl," he whispered, and she moved against him in a way that reminded him of a kitten looking to be stroked.

She liked it, he realized.

She liked his praise, and she responded to his commanding tone. Her gaze held a bit of adoration, and that made him want to get on his knees and worship her in turn. He didn't know exactly what she'd been through, but enough to know that her trust was fragile and precious. And she was trusting him to be in charge of her body without taking advantage. To be firm with her without hurting her.

Bloody hell, she was too perfect for words, and what she was offering him—the trust and the faith and the sweet innocence…

It humbled him to his very core.

"Do you know why your apologies bother me?" he asked, his lips close to her ear.

She shook her head, her hips rocking slightly between his palm, which was cupping her quim in a firm grip and his other hand, which was still clutching her bottom.

"Because your pleasure is my greatest triumph," he said.

She pulled back to meet his gaze, confusion and disbelief there.

"I mean it. I want you to trust me to touch you." He leaned forward to nip at her lips. "It is my right and my honor as your husband to teach you just how much pleasure you can experience."

"What sort of pleasure?" she asked.

He whispered against her lips. "I'll show you."

Go slow, he reminded himself, even though he ached everywhere to be closer to her sweet heat. And so, he did not take her the way he wanted, but he maneuvered his hand between her thighs so that even though the material was a barrier, his fingers were parting her folds.

She moaned into his neck, and he nearly came in his trousers at the feel of her.

"You're so very wet for me," he said.

"And that's good?" Her voice was high, and it broke with a whimper when he moved his fingers, sliding them back and forth between her thighs. He couldn't wait to feel the silky slick heat of her inner folds, but for now, he settled for touching her through the wet material, using its friction to tease her sensitive skin.

"That is very, very good, my little love." His fingers were coated with her juices, the fabric soaked as he rubbed that tight nub at the apex of her womanhood and then stroked inward until his fingertips were dipping into her channel.

She was writhing now, pressing her pert tits into his chest as she sought out something she didn't even know how to name.

"That's right, my little kitten," he growled into her ear. "You move your hips and you ride my fingers until you find what you need. That's my good girl."

His words of encouragement had her writhing even more, and he couldn't keep his other hand still. He dragged it upward from her tight little bottom to her waist and then up further until he was cupping her breast as he buried his face in the crook of her neck, sucking on her sweet skin as her hips bucked wildly.

"Is this all right?" he teased as his fingers found her hard nub and pinched.

Her hips bucked wildly as she moaned and whimpered. He moved his fingers more aggressively now, helping her to find the friction and the rhythm that she needed. When she pulled back and kissed him so sweetly, he sought out her clitoris and rubbed it hard and fast until she was panting against his lips. "What is...I can't..."

"Shh," he soothed. "You can and you will, love."

Her gaze met his and it was filled with questions and confusion as she lost control over her body. He knew what she needed. She needed him to take control, to give her permission, and tell her what to do.

"That's it, love," he growled. "You look into my eyes, and you let me watch."

When he slid his thick middle finger toward her tight channel, the tip of it nudging inside of her, he felt her muscles there contracting, pulsing…

"Let me see you come for me, kitten," he growled. "Be a good girl and show your husband how you like it. Show me the pleasure I make you feel."

Her hips jerked, and he pressed his thumb to her rhythmically, matching her rhythm as she ground down against his hand.

"Come for me," he commanded.

Her lips parted and her eyes widened with surprise as the first wave of orgasm crashed into her. And then she was falling into his arms, letting him hold her and stroke her until the last wave subsided and she lay there, panting in his arms.

CHAPTER NINE

O H GOODNESS. SO that was what all the fuss was about.

Madeline's head rested against Hayden's shoulder, and she had no concept of how much time passed, only that she was lulled into a blissful state of half-sleep as he stroked her hair and her back, her thighs and her cheek.

He stroked her for so long and with such care, she found herself wondering if she'd died and gone to heaven.

And, apparently, she said it aloud, because she felt his low chuckle through his chest beneath her cheek. "Not heaven, love. Though right now, I feel as though I've found my very own angel."

She smiled shyly. When at last she had the energy to move, she pulled back to find him gazing down at her with the kindest smile she'd ever seen. Her heart gave a painful thud that seemed to steal her breath.

"May I?" he asked.

She wasn't sure what he meant, but a second later, he scooped her up into his arms and carried her over to the bed. He joined her.

Oh.

Oh.

His chuckle was low and warm. "No, no. I don't want to see that fear returning. Not around me."

Her lips quirked up. Had she looked scared? She supposed she was…a little. But not like she'd been before. The way he'd touched her…

His gentleness, the unselfishness, and the consideration for her feelings. It had helped her to forget those vile men who'd made her feel so ashamed of her body and dread a man's touch.

"I'm not afraid, necessarily," she said slowly as he turned onto his side beside her, stretching out as his free hand trailed idly over her arm and then her belly, like he had all the time in the world to explore her.

Like there was no rush whatsoever.

If it weren't for the rather difficult-to-ignore bulge in his trousers, she might have believed he didn't care in the least if she spread her legs for him.

"What…" She started and then stopped. "What should I do?"

Amusement flickered in his eyes, but she didn't feel as though he was laughing at her. "You, my dear, don't have to do anything. It's a man's duty to ensure that his woman is ready to take him."

"T-take him?"

"Mmm." His murmur was a growl that seemed to rumble low in his chest as he leaned over her, his lips so close, all she had to do was strain upward and they were meeting again. Molding together in that way that felt so very blissful.

He kissed her long and slow, until she was mindless with sensations. And it wasn't until his body was pressed along the length of hers that she realized he'd been slowly, oh so slowly, lowering himself on top of her.

He was careful about not scaring her, and that only made her response to him heighten. Her skin seemed to spark with sensations wherever his touch roamed. And that tension she'd thought was gone returned tenfold low in her belly, making her squirm and wriggle, seeking out that heady relief he'd given her before.

"I want to see you, love," he whispered against her neck when her legs spread for him, when her hips arched.

She held her breath when his hand came to the buttons on her gown.

He noticed. Of course, he did. No one had ever paid such singular attention to her in all her life.

"No?" he said. There was no pleading there, no hint of disappointment. It was just a question, and there was no wrong answer.

"No," she whispered.

He dropped a whisper of a kiss on the tip of her ear. "One day," he said.

It didn't sound like a threat, but rather like a promise. Like he understood, somehow, and that he would help her to overcome all the bad that had been done to her.

She was grateful, so touched, she drew in a deep breath and reached for the bottom of the nightdress. She could not bring herself to bare her body completely. The mere thought had her mind filling with the stench of cigar smoke and the sight of dark, cruel eyes.

She shivered as she swept the thought away. They were not here, and thanks to this man, they would never see her again.

Her fingers grasped the frilly lace edge and tugged up as William stilled above her.

William.

She liked that name. She liked that she was free to use it. It felt so very intimate. Nearly as intimate as what she was about to do.

Swallowing hard, she focused on his eyes, which were heavy on her—eager, excited, lustful…but concerned. For her.

Lord, but she'd been so lucky to find this man. Or rather, that he'd found her.

Her hands began to shake, but she did not stop hitching up her skirts until she was bare below the waist.

She saw his jaw work as he shed his trousers, and when his pulsing manhood met her wet, swollen sex, they both let out a moan.

But for a long moment, he didn't move, and she saw the strain in his eyes and around his mouth as he held still, giving her time to adjust to this new sensation of skin against skin. Of her most sensitive, intimate place pressing against his.

He was wedged between her thighs, and that hard shaft prodded against her, but still, he did not move.

Instead, he lifted one of his hands to cup her cheek. "Wife," he gritted out through that clenched jaw. "You are my wife."

She nodded, understanding what he was trying to say. That this was not wrong, nor embarrassing. That this might hurt but that it was right and good.

"Yes," she whispered.

His hips rocked a bit, widening her thighs to make room for him.

She swallowed hard and watched as possessive need clouded his gaze. The last time she'd seen that look it had scared her. It had reminded her too much of the way her father's eyes would cloud over just before one of his fits.

My untouched daughter. No man will defile you.

She gave her head a shake. This was no time to be thinking about her father's madness or those men who'd defiled her with their hands and their eyes.

He moved his hand down to grip her chin, forcing her to meet his gaze. To return to him in the here and now.

"I am the only man who touches you," he said.

She nodded, swallowing hard. This time that dark, possessive heat in his eyes didn't scare her. This time it made her feel protected. He would not let her father or those men touch her ever again.

"You are mine," he said. "My wife."

"Yes," she whispered.

He pressed his forehead to hers as he pushed his shaft inside her. Slowly at first, pausing each time her breath hitched to let her adjust.

She wasn't sure time would help. Surely, he would never fit.

He kissed her forehead, her nose, her cheeks. "Christ, you're so tight," he muttered. "So tight and so wet for me."

She felt heat spike in her cheeks. He'd said not to be embarrassed, but it still seemed so odd how her body reacted to his touch. Even now, when he felt hard and big inside her, the pressure uncomfortable to the point of pain, she was still keenly aware of how good his hands felt.

After a few moments, her knees fell apart, opening for him.

He groaned, trailing kisses down her neck in praise.

"This will hurt, love, but I promise you after the pain there will be more pleasure." He nipped at her ear. "Do you believe me?"

"Yes."

He stilled at the quickness of her answer. "Do you trust me?"

The moment felt weighted, as if her answer meant everything to him.

She buried her fingers in his hair, a bold move that felt very intimate. Also…empowering. He was hers to touch just as she was his to bed. She nodded, tears choking her for a moment as she realized the truth of it. "Yes, I trust you."

He growled his pleasure as he withdrew and then plowed into her.

She cried out at the sharp pain, her head arching back and her hips jerked in some primal need to get away. But when he stilled again, tense and frozen above her, she started to calm. Her heart rate slowed as she focused on the feel of his breath, harsh and ragged against her neck.

The pain between her legs began to fade as she adjusted to him.

"I'm sorry, love," he said. His voice sounded different. Harsh and…pained. He *was* in pain, she realized. Staying still like this was causing him pain.

The thought had her cradling his head in her hands, and she tugged him back so she could see his face.

He looked like he was steeling himself for battle. Like he was bracing himself for torture.

"I'm okay," she whispered. She nudged her hips, and indeed…she was okay.

It was not a pleasant sensation, but the pain was gone, leaving only pressure and an odd new tightness. But she could feel her inner muscles adjusting, making room for him.

His mouth claimed hers in a brutal kiss as he moved, slowly at first. And then she kissed him back eagerly, with more urgency.

In and out he slid, that thick member filling her over and over until she started to welcome the feel of him so deep inside her.

She shocked them both when she lifted her knees and arched her hips to take him further.

"Christ, love, you feel so good," he growled into her ear.

She shivered and wrapped her arms around him to pull him closer still. When he shifted, wedging a hand between them, she started to protest. She liked the feel of his hard chest pressing her into the bed. There was something comforting about his weight, like his body was a shield between her and the bad memories. Between her and everyone who'd ever done her harm.

But then his clever fingers found that swollen nub he'd been stroking earlier, and her body reacted to his touch like kindling to a spark.

Her whole body tensed when he stroked her there and her inner muscles tightened as if trying to keep him inside of her longer.

"That's it," he said as he timed his thrusts with his strokes. "Take it deep, love. Take all of me like the good girl you are."

She moaned and whimpered as he teased her, his praise-filled voice soothing her nerves and her thoughts. The pain and the pressure were forgotten as she did as he commanded, welcoming his thrusts as his fingers worked magic along her slick skin.

"I'm going to fill you with my seed." His low growl next to her ear made her shiver. "I'm going to get you with child. My child."

He was murmuring the words as if caught in a fever. If so, it was contagious, because she felt it, too. This fervent, senseless need to be joined. To make this permanent. To belong.

"Yes," she hissed. The thought of him filling her with a child had her head falling back, and she lifted her knees, taking him as deep as she could.

"Just like that, love," he said. "You know just how to take your husband, don't you?"

"Yes," she breathed. And she did. It was like some primal part of her understood this act and craved it.

"Will you come for me, my little love?" he growled against her lips. "Will you take my cock deep inside you and come all over it like a good girl?"

"Yes," she was whining now. She didn't even understand the words, but she knew the meaning.

And when his hands gripped her hips and held her down so he could ram his rod deep inside her, she threw her head back and shouted her pleasure. His fingers circled her nub with furious strokes, and she couldn't fight it. She didn't want to.

She let him lead her to that furious release, and this time was even better because when her inner muscles clenched and tightened, she was full, so very full…of her husband.

A second later he growled incoherently, and his thrusts grew fast and hard until she felt him spurt hot liquid inside her before falling on top of her with words of praise.

"So perfect, love. You are so bloody perfect," he murmured.

She was dimly aware of him pulling out of her a moment later. She lifted her hands to try and bring him back, but her eyes refused to open.

She didn't feel safe without his weight.

How odd. From going her whole life on her own, to needing someone else just to feel safe.

But then again, maybe she'd never felt safe before.

Before Hayden.

Her husband.

The thought didn't send her into a panic this time but had her smiling against the pillow.

He was back a moment later, and Madeline felt a warm rag cleaning her thighs.

She ought to protest. She ought to be embarrassed. But sleep had dug its claws in, and she felt him lay beside her and tug her into his arms just as sleep took her under.

She awoke sometime later to the feel of his hard length digging into her bottom, his arm a heavy weight over her waist. She gasped and stiffened.

It took her a moment to realize where she was.

"Are you all right?" His voice was gruff and sleepy.

"Yes," she said, forcing herself to relax. "I just…I've never slept with someone before."

His low chuckle had her dipping her head into the pillow with a silly smile. "You know what I mean."

Odd how something could feel so bizarre and unfamiliar…and yet so wonderfully right all at the same time.

She snuggled into his embrace, wiggling her hips a bit to get comfortable. The thick protrusion against her bottom swelled in response. She gasped, which made him chuckle again.

He dropped a kiss on the top of her shoulder. "Don't worry, love. I know you're too sore for another round."

Was she? She wriggled again and winced. Yes, she supposed she was.

He groaned. "I'd beg you to stop wiggling your bottom like that. I'm trying to be a gentleman here, but my willpower is only so strong around you."

She grinned because she didn't believe him for a moment. "I don't think you do yourself credit," she whispered. "I trust you not to hurt me."

He sighed, and she felt his smile against her neck. "I love that you trust me. I can't imagine trust comes easily for you."

"With you it does." She turned her head. "Why is that?"

She could see the laughter in his eyes, even in this dim light with only a low fire crackling in the hearth.

"Why? Well, I suppose because I swept into your life like some prince in a fairytale."

She giggled at his teasing. "Swept in, did you? I thought it was more like…stumbled through my window reeking of liquor."

His chuckle warmed her from head to toe.

"You have your story and I have mine."

She found his hand against her waist and squeezed it. "No matter what brought you there or how it came about, I am so very grateful you came for me."

He was quiet for a long moment. "I don't want your gratitude, Madeline."

"Then what do you want?" The question came bursting out of her, and she wished she could call it back. She wasn't sure she wanted to know the answer.

But he went quiet again, for so long she wondered if maybe he'd fallen asleep. But then he squeezed her tight. "Get some sleep. Tonight is the start of a new life for you. And I have it on good authority that new lives require much rest."

She smiled at his teasing tone. "Is that right?"

"Mmm."

She started to think about what the next day would bring and some of her giddiness faded into nerves. "I'm afraid."

Something she wasn't sure she would have admitted if she were facing him in broad daylight. But it was dark, and he was a warm, strong, a reassuring presence at her back.

"Of being a marchioness?"

She nodded.

"My housekeeper and the butler, all the servants…they will be overjoyed to teach you all there is to know of this estate."

She nodded again. "That's nice of them."

"But that's not all that worries you."

She shook her head. "It's being out there that scares me."

What a foolish thing to say. And yet he seemed to understand. He burrowed his face against her neck with a long exhale. "My beautiful wife, you've been kept away from the world for too long. You deserve to be seen and heard. You ought to be shared with the world, for to hide you away is a disservice to others."

Her eyes brimmed with tears, but she smiled all the same, and her laugh when it escaped was genuine. "You are very kind to me."

"You deserve kindness," he said simply.

So simply. Like it was the truth.

And maybe…maybe it was. Her eyes started to drift as she let this new idea wash over her.

He kissed her neck. "Get some rest, love."

Maybe this was what she deserved…

Or maybe this was all much too good to be true.

CHAPTER TEN

I F IT WEREN'T for her husband's hand on her back, Madeline was certain she'd be swept away by the crowd.

William's voice was low and right next to her ear as he leaned over her protectively. "Are you all right?"

She nodded but couldn't quite say "yes." Would he even hear her if she were to speak anyway? She doubted it.

The lobby of the opera house was packed with lords and ladies, their laughter and chatter filling the air until it seemed the high, arched ceiling might explode from it all.

Or perhaps she was the only one who would explode. Or be crushed.

It was a toss-up.

"We just have to make our way over there," William said, nudging her toward an archway leading to a set of stairs. "That's the way to Raff's box."

Nodding, she gritted her teeth. She could do this. It was important to William. And to her, she supposed. He was right about her needing to attend society events at some point or another. And the opera, he'd decided, would be the best way to start.

She wouldn't need to speak to many people, he'd informed her. It would only be Raff and Evangeline in the box with them, and the rest of society would be kept at bay.

"They will gape and stare, I'm afraid," he'd warned her tonight before they set out, holding her gloved hand in his so gently, as if she were made of glass. "But at least you will not be forced to make endless small talk and answer their ill-disguised questions."

"Ill-disguised questions?" she'd echoed.

He winced. "I'm afraid there will be much speculation about you. And your father," he'd said slowly.

She could handle it. If they could just make it to the duke's box without her being crushed or fainting over the sheer amount of people and voices, she planned to prove just that.

Soon enough, they reached the stairway, but not before she'd overheard Hayden's title spoken dozens of times. Whispers and stares followed in their wake, and she did not miss the myriad of questions that seemed to whirl about her.

Who is she? When did they wed? How did they meet?

Is she really the mad earl's daughter?

I was told she didn't exist.

William paused just beyond a curtain that separated them from most of the crowd in the lobby. "How are you faring?" His gaze raked over her before she could respond.

She managed a nod and what she hoped to be a smile.

It might have been more like a grimace. But it was enough to have the line of tension easing from between his brows. "That's my girl," he murmured as he lifted her gloved hands to his lips. "Raff's box is just through there," he said. "And from here on out, if they whisper, we won't be able to hear it."

She laughed despite her tension. "That sounds lovely."

But it did make her wonder how long the whispers would last, and if, perhaps, there was something she ought to be doing to put them to rest.

With her brother away and her father bedridden, it fell to her to make excuses for her upbringing—to explain why she'd been hidden away. Hayden and his friends had offered up options. That she'd been unwell as a child or off traveling with an aunt.

She'd opted for the former. It was closer to the truth and

would require less imaginative responses than if anyone were to ask where she'd traveled and what she'd seen.

If she merely said she'd been unwell and kept to her chambers, it wasn't as though anyone would refute that. Hayden assured her the countess wouldn't. And besides, the countess was nearly as isolated from society as her father had been these last few years. Aside from her newfound friendship with that snake Mr. Foley, of course—a man Madeline had since learned knew no limits to his knavery.

She did not think the countess would be so bitter as to reveal her illegitimate status now after all these years. But then again, she'd never claimed her as her daughter to the rest of the world, only to their father when he'd demanded it.

"What are you fretting about, love?" William asked.

She tried to smile. "Just wondering about the countess and…" She waved a hand. "About what people will say…"

He stopped walking to turn and face her, his fingers pinching her chin gently as he brought her face up to meet his gaze. "You need not worry about what that woman says. Nor what people whisper or assume." He smiled broadly. "There are some perks to marrying a marquess, you know. And a wealthy one at that."

She laughed at his teasing. It was impossible not to when his eyes gleamed with amusement as they did now.

"Your troubles are mine now," he said. "She can't hurt you or me so long as we stand together. Do you understand?"

She nodded, but her lungs hitched with newfound emotions. She ought to be used to it by now. They'd been married a week, and each day she was struck anew with these waves of gratitude and happiness and…the fear that always accompanied them both. The whisper in her ear told her this new life was too good to be true.

And tonight, she was able to put a name and face to her fears. It was the countess's voice she heard. It was the countess's cold eyes she imagined each time she felt too happy.

Because surely the countess would not stand idly by and

allow her illegitimate daughter, whom she despised, to have so much joy. Not when her plans had been thwarted by Madeline's happy match.

She'd learned enough from William to know that he had not given her all she'd asked. And what the countess had asked wasn't even close to the amount she'd hoped to gain by auctioning Madeline off to the highest bidder.

William smiled down at her and offered his arm. "Ready?"

She nodded, and indeed some of her tension eased at the thought of being alone with William and his friends.

His friends who were starting to become her friends, as well.

And so yes, perhaps William had a point. She wasn't alone anymore. And she wasn't the hated, unwanted girl stuck in a tower either. She was a marchioness now, and she could count a duchess as one of her friends in life.

Surely that was something.

And besides, when Albert returned, he'd know how to speak to the countess. The two didn't exactly have a warm, familial bond—Madeline wasn't sure the countess was capable of such a thing—but if she cared about anyone, it was Albert. So, he alone could persuade her.

Once inside the box, she was too distracted by Evangeline's embrace and Raff's warm greeting to worry about anything at all. And when William helped her to her seat and sat beside her, explaining to her the different instruments in the orchestra below the stage, and the story behind the opera they were about to see, she was far too entertained to care.

And then the music swelled, and the curtain rose, and Madeline...

Madeline was transported.

She'd heard about operas from Albert, and he'd even read her some plays he'd found in her father's study. But she'd never dreamed it could be like this.

William squeezed her hand when the first opera singer opened her mouth...and then the magic truly began. Madeline's heart was lost as the sound swept over her. The voice, the music, the emotions that struck her deep inside even though she did not know the words.

She could not look away even as the scenery was being changed. Indeed, even the set and the workers seemed to be a part of this magic. All combined, the people and the music and the stage…

"It's a miracle," she whispered.

She turned to see if William was just as smitten, but his gaze was fixed on her. She realized during the next scene that his attention was more on her, and his gaze was filled with affection. Never in her life had she felt more cherished.

Emotions got the best of her, and she swiped away a tear when the intermission came about.

"What do you think, darling?" William asked.

"Thank you." She reached for his arm and squeezed. "Thank you for bringing me here. For showing me this…"

She trailed off as she shook her head. She didn't even have the words.

His chuckle was low in his throat. "It is my pleasure, love. Trust me, I have never been more entertained during a night at the theater."

She grinned at his teasing. "Am I making a spectacle of myself?"

"Not at all." He reached out and brushed away the last of her tears. "I'm honored that I could be here for your first time." His grin grew wolfish. "For all your first times."

She gasped, clasping her lips together tight as her cheeks filled with heat, which made William laugh all over again.

"Raff and I will go fetch you ladies something to drink," he said. "Stay here and let all those preening peacocks below wonder at what has you blushing so."

She giggled. "You're terrible."

But he and Raff were soon gone, and she made the mistake of looking out at the aforementioned preening peacocks. "Oh dear," she whispered.

Evangeline shifted closer. "Just ignore them, dear. Better yet, look at me and smile."

"Like this?" Madeline's smile turned genuine when she met Evangeline's laughing gaze.

"Yes, just like that," she said. "Now wave your fan and pretend I said something amusing."

Madeline didn't have to pretend to laugh. Her laughter helped to ease her fears. "Thank you, Evangeline. I'm so grateful for you, Raff, and the others."

Evangeline tsked. "It's our pleasure. You are a lovely addition to our little circle. And, I must confess…" She leaned forward, and Madeline did the same. "We've all found it quite diverting to watch dear Hayden fall in love."

Madeline drew back with a start. "Oh, but…but it's not like that."

Evangeline bit her lip, clearly trying not to laugh. "Is it not? Do you know, Benedict said that Hayden has barely touched a drink since he discovered you."

Hadn't he? Come to think of it, Madeline hadn't seen him imbibe much either, aside from some wine with dinner. "Is that so very odd?"

Evangeline studied her. "Perhaps not. If you'll forgive me, your husband always struck me as rather a…" She shrugged. "A lost soul, I suppose. He had his friends, of course, but he seemed rather lonely all the same. You've been good for him."

Madeline knew she ought to drop it. But she heard herself say, "How?"

Evangeline's eyes widened. "Well…" She tilted her head to the side as if giving it serious thought. "I think sometimes a man needs a purpose in life. He needs responsibilities and…and someone to take care of."

Madeline nodded slowly, the words sifting and sorting in her mind as she turned them over.

Evangeline winced. "I'm sorry. That didn't come out right."

"No, no," Madeline said. "I think I know what you meant." She'd seen it, too, of course. The way William had seemed to come into his own right before her eyes. How he'd gained a sense of determination and…and calm. Like he was content.

Was that because of her?

Had he needed someone to love? Someone to take care of?

The thought made her chest ache in a way that was bittersweet. She liked the way he cared for her. She loved it, really. Never in her life had she known such affection and tenderness. Never had anyone looked after her like she was worthy of being loved.

She swallowed hard, realizing that Evangeline still watched her.

"He has been wonderful to me," she said slowly. "Kind and patient and…I do not know that I deserve him."

I do not trust that it will last.

She didn't say it aloud, but she could have sworn Evangeline heard it, because her friend reached out and grasped her hand, squeezing it tight.

"You deserve happiness, just as he does," she said.

Madeline smiled. She believed that William deserved all the best. And she wanted that for him. She wished she could take care of him like he did her. But how?

She hadn't the training to help him manage his marquessate. She was no fine lady nor a beguiling hostess. So far, she'd brought him little but trouble.

Her thoughts scattered as she turned back to the crowded seats below. Oh goodness. For a moment there she'd forgotten how much attention she'd drawn.

So many stares.

She wet her lips, ignoring the rapid beat of her heart as nerves swept over her. She ought to just ignore the stares like William and Evangeline said.

But a nagging sensation had her turning in her seat. She could feel a set of eyes on her, and the moment she caught the man staring, her stomach turned with a violent jolt.

It was him. The man with the oily beard who'd been there that night.

His lips curved in a sneer as he met her gaze with a dark glower.

A shudder of horror rippled through her as all the memories she'd thought to forget came rushing back. This man and his calloused hands pawing at her. He and the other men squeezing her breasts like she was fruit at the market. The foul stench of cigar smoke and the coarse, lewd words they used to describe parts of her body.

Bile rose up and burned the back of her mouth. She clapped a hand over her lips just in time. How had it not occurred to her that she might see them again? That they would see her?

It had been wishful thinking at its worst. She'd gotten too comfortable in Hayden's home, had started to believe his words that her past was well behind her.

It wasn't. It was here. Now.

And it was staring right at her.

"Madeline, are you all right?" Evangeline's voice seemed to carry from far away.

And then Madeline was rushing toward the curtains and into the hallway. She just needed a moment of privacy. A second away from that awful leer.

"Aw, if it isn't the little damsel in distress herself." Foley's voice greeted her in the hallway.

She stopped short with a gasp. "What are you doing here?"

"Why, enjoying the opera, of course." His smile didn't reach his eyes.

Madeline looked toward the lobby, the sounds from which were loud even from here.

"My husband will be returning any moment, and if he catches you—"

"I would not make threats if I were you. You are in no position to see them through." His voice was cold, and he did not even feign a smile any longer. "Besides, I was sent here by your mother."

She is not my mother. Madeline just barely swallowed the words. No one could know that, could they? She certainly couldn't be heard admitting it. Not if she didn't want to bring even more scandal upon William and his title.

Foley tsked and wagged a finger. "Naughty, naughty girl. I'm still not sure how you managed to win over a marquess while locked away in that tower, but mark my words, the countess will not forgive and forget."

"I didn't—"

"You think to cheat her—and me—out of the fortune we were promised by those wealthy gentlemen, but you are mistaken."

Madeline shook her head, her stomach churning dangerously. "She had no authority to…to sell me like I was some—"

"Illegitimate bastard?" he finished, his voice cruel and cold. "But that's precisely what you are. And since the countess was good enough to raise you as a daughter, she is your guardian. She had every right to sell you off to whoever she wanted you." His smile was salacious and awful. "And they surely wanted you, Madeline, could you not tell?"

She backed away but ended up running into the wall.

His gaze flickered toward the lobby. "Now, we haven't much time. But rest assured, your mother has devised a way for you to make this up to her."

"But I haven't—"

"Hush, child," he scolded. "After all, you wouldn't want your new husband to know what loose morals you have, would you?"

Her lips parted but nothing came out.

"No, of course not," he finished with a smug smirk.

"Loose morals," she finally sputtered. "But I did nothing—"

"Didn't you?" he said idly. "Why, dirty little whore that you are, you let all those men see you naked." He looked horrified. "You let them touch you."

She recoiled at the harsh words, her stomach churning with guilt and shame as the memories reared up. "I did not condone—"

"You didn't protest either, though, now did you?"

"I—I—" She wanted to say she had, but she'd been too frightened, and all too aware that her mother was standing there sanctioning their horrid acts.

She'd been powerless.

"Besides, who would believe you? You're just as mad as your father." He leaned in. "Everyone knows the marquess doesn't trust women, especially not loose ones like you."

"But I never—"

"I've got plenty of men who will say that you wanted it. That you were a tease and a whore and a—"

The slap of her hand across his cheek sounded sickeningly loud. But as her hand dropped and a red mark appeared on his cheek, he merely smiled.

"You think a slap will stop me? Or the countess? Stupid, foolish little girl. You have no idea how much I'd love to tear the marquess's world apart. He and his friends have laughed at me and scorned me and..." He broke off with an oath. "I assure you it would be a pleasure to destroy his marriage. But—" He held his hands out meekly, with a pale imitation of an indulgent smile. "I'm afraid your mother wants his money more than revenge."

"Money? But he's already—"

They both stopped speaking when they heard voices coming toward the box.

"I'll be in touch, girl. Don't weep and whine to the marquess, if you please. I'll only have to destroy the marriage and then your mother would be very unhappy indeed."

He flashed her a wicked grin before turning and disappearing into an alcove.

"Why, Madeline, what are you doing out here?" William smiled at her a moment later as he handed her a glass of champagne.

"I...I..." Her head whirled as Foley's words raced in her head.

"I just needed some air."

He smiled kindly and caught her arm. "Come, let's have a seat before the second act begins."

She nodded, following blindly.

Would William believe Foley if we carried through with his threat? Or would William threaten the man and end up in a duel? Scenario after scenario played out, ones in which William believed Foley's lies and ones in which he didn't.

None were good, though.

William deserved so much better than any of them. Even if he believed her, she dreaded the look in his eyes when he looked at her knowing how she'd been touched.

How she'd let them touch her. Because Foley was right. She hadn't protested. She hadn't fought back.

The second act was nothing but a blur.

And by the time they left, she knew one thing for certain. She could not tell her husband about that night.

CHAPTER ELEVEN

WILLIAM OBSERVED HIS wife as she stared out the carriage window.

Staring at his wife seemed to have become his new favorite pastime. She was beautiful, there was that. So gorgeous, and more so with each new day that she ate and slept well. But it was more than that. It was seeing the emotions play out across her face. The way her eyes lit with pleasure each time she saw something new.

And it seemed like every hour she came upon something new. A stroll around the neighborhood, a visit to a tea shop. Each seemingly ordinary outing had been a burst of new sensations for his bride.

And seeing the world like that through her eyes—everything new and sweet and wonderful…

Well, it made him feel like a new man.

Truly, he'd never known such happiness as he had since marrying. His days were filled with showing Madeline all she'd been missing, or conversing over meals, or helping her learn the duties that would be expected of her.

And their nights…

A smile tugged at his lips as he memorized her profile. Their nights were sublime. He'd never known it could be like this. So overwhelming. The connection so intimate.

But there were moments… Moments like this one when he felt that connection sever. When he was certain they were living two different lives and he did not know her at all. She'd been distant for hours now. She'd gone from being so entranced by the opera to seemingly distracted.

Was she hiding something from him?

He shook his head. That was his sordid history at work, making him suspicious. It was not reality. She was too guileless and sweet to be untrustworthy. But even so…

He shifted uneasily. She still wouldn't bare herself in front of him, not even in bed. She welcomed him into her bed and was an enthusiastic lover. But there were limits. She would not be naked in front of him, and there were things he did that made her quake with fear.

He'd stop whenever she grew frightened, of course. And he'd tried time and again to get her to talk to him about what it was that scared her so. He hoped that, in time, she'd explain.

She would, he told himself as the carriage stopped in front of his home. He just had to be patient, that was all.

He offered her a hand out. "Are you certain you're well?"

She blinked up at him as if surprised to see him there. Then she flashed a brilliant smile. "Yes. Yes, of course."

"Of course," he muttered. A muscle in his jaw tensed. He did not want to push, but he was nearly certain she'd just lied to him.

And lying he could not abide.

"Actually…" She cleared her throat, pausing to smile graciously at the butler and housekeeper who came to greet them. "I'm not feeling well," she said to him with a little wince of regret.

A surge of guilt reared up, for doubting her and for tiring her out so. He'd been pushing her too hard and too fast this week. "Perhaps we ought to draw you a bath," he said.

She nodded. "That would be lovely."

He watched her disappear with the housekeeper before wandering into his study. A decanter was open, and its contents tempted. He'd been a veritable saint these past two weeks, too focused on taking care of Madeline to waste precious time being in his cups…or suffering the aftermath.

Truthfully, he'd discovered that whiling away the hours in his wife's bed was far more pleasant than imbibing home alone or a night out at one of Vestry Lane's tawdry gaming hells and brothels.

He sank into his seat, a daft smile on his lips as he thought of all the ways he could while away the hours tonight. But then he remembered how quiet she'd been on the ride home and his smile faltered.

Perhaps he ought to let her rest.

He reached for the decanter and poured himself a glass. He likely *was* pushing her too much, and not just by taking her out on the town. He had to give her time to adjust.

She was so eager and responsive in bed, sometimes it was easy to forget that she'd been an innocent only days ago.

He threw back the drink far too quickly.

It did little to calm his tense muscles. Pinching the bridge of his nose, his mind fixated on the way she'd lied earlier.

Likely nothing. Maybe she really had been feeling under the weather and hadn't wanted to admit it straight away.

Of course that was it. Madeline was many things, but she was no liar.

He poured another glass. He could feel them stirring, those memories best left in the past.

Madeline was nothing like his traitorous stepmother. That woman had been a flirt and a slattern, although she'd hidden it well in the beginning.

His own mother…God rest her soul. She'd been sweet and docile. She'd loved him, at least, as a mother should. But she'd given him up to run off with another man. He'd always told himself she would have come back for him if she hadn't died so soon amidst the scandal.

But his stepmother—she'd fooled them all in the beginning.

So confident and witty, entertaining and clever. So lively and vivacious, and nothing at all like his quiet, timid mother. And his stepmother had been as hungry for power as his father had been.

They'd deserved each other, he supposed. Lord knew his father wasn't faithful, not to either wife. But after his father's first wife left him...well, he'd turned mean to both his son and his new wife.

Hayden hadn't particularly minded. He'd never liked his father, let alone loved him. There'd always been a cold distance between them, which had only grown worse after his mother's betrayal. But the new marchioness did not take to the old marquess's harsh words so well. She'd set off to make a cuckold of his father, and she'd succeeded mightily.

Until the night she'd decided to make a cuckold of her husband with her own stepson.

Hayden slammed the glass down.

His father was dead, and the dowager marchioness had long since been driven off to find another man with another title...and even more fortune, no doubt.

And none of that had anything to do with his wife. Madeline wasn't manipulative and she'd never lied. Just because she had her secrets did not mean she was untrustworthy.

He leaned forward. The drink had been a bad idea. It only made his head pound and trudged up memories he didn't care to address.

What he needed was to focus on the present and his future.

On his wife.

The first part of this evening had been one of the best moments of his life. He'd never seen anything more moving than Madeline responding to the music.

Such a soulful creature. So much heart and goodness. And all of it his to protect and cherish.

That humbling sensation had him getting up and out, away from the liquor and the haunting past and out to find his wife.

Surely she'd be done bathing by now. And he couldn't wait

one more moment to have her in his arms.

His wife. A woman he could trust and care for and protect and…

And love.

He nearly stumbled over his own two feet. He paused with one hand on the banister. Was this what all his friends had been babbling on about these past months?

A grin split his face, and his mind called up the image of his beautiful bride crying as she watched the opera tonight.

His own heart swelled to the point of bursting.

This was love.

He choked on a laugh that caught him by surprise.

Good Lord. He loved his wife.

And he suspected…maybe she'd love him, too. One day. If he gave her the time and the space she needed. He started walking up the stairs again, his heart slamming against his ribcage with this revelation.

He wouldn't tell her yet. She wasn't ready. But he'd continue doing what seemed to make her happiest. Bringing her out of the shadows and into the light. Helping her to see just how wonderful she was and all that she deserved.

He wanted to see her respond to art again and a new idea took hold.

The National Gallery. Tomorrow, he'd take her there to view the paintings. They'd go when the crowd was minimal, and if the weather was nice enough, he'd have the cook prepare a picnic for the park afterward.

He smiled as he strode up to her bedroom. But with a quick glance inside her room, he realized that she was still bathing in the adjacent dressing room.

He paced for long moments, staring at the closed door, beyond which his lovely wife was no doubt naked.

And wet.

Oh hell. The mere thought had his manhood straining and wondering just how wrong it would be to go in there. The angel on his shoulder said give her space. The devil was crying out for him to kick the bloody door down and drag his wife into his arms.

With a curse, he decided to remove himself from temptation.

She'd seemed disturbed tonight, there was no doubt about it. And if his sweet, trusting wife needed some time alone to sift through all she'd seen and heard this evening, then so be it.

He headed for the door but turned back at the last moment. He was still eager to tell her about his plans for the morning—perhaps the adventure would cheer her.

And besides, he hadn't gone to sleep without wishing her goodnight since they'd wed.

His gaze fell on the writing desk by the window. He'd just write her a brief note, that was all. He'd wish her a good rest and tell her he'd see her at first light and—

And his hand fell on a piece of paper atop the untouched parchment. He pulled it out and he meant to set it aside, but before he could, his gaze caught on words, urgent and sickening.

You must help me. I was forced into marriage. I do not want to be wed to the marquess. Save me, please.

CHAPTER TWELVE

MADELINE DALLIED TOO long in the bathtub. The water was cold when she finally stepped out, but she sent her maid away before she could help her dress.

William was in her room.

She'd heard him come in, and he hadn't left. He was waiting for her. And tonight was the night. She hastily tossed on her night-rail before she could lose her nerve.

Her husband had been patient. More than patient. He'd been supportive and kind, and…

And the least she could do was try to open up to him. To let him in.

There shouldn't be barriers between a man and wife. At least, not if this was to be a true partnership. And that was what she wanted.

And she suspected he did, too.

She opened the door cautiously, her heart hammering. Perhaps she was too late. Maybe he'd already gone to his rooms.

But then she spotted him, sitting on the edge of her bed, his elbows resting on his knees and his head bowed.

She took another step in, and this time he heard her. His head came up with a snap.

The intensity in his eyes stole her breath. The hunger there made her belly tighten, heat pooling between her thighs in anticipation.

"Feeling better?" he asked.

There was something off about his voice. It was gruff and low, but…cold.

He didn't sound anything like his normal warm self.

She shivered. But she wasn't about to back out of her plan now. She would reveal herself to her husband—in every sense of the word, physically and emotionally.

He stood, and he looked like he was about to speak, but he stopped when she started to undress.

Her fingers trembled, and for a moment his confusion and shock were almost amusing.

Almost. They would have been if she wasn't so very afraid.

This is William, she told herself. *Your husband*. There was nothing to fear. But her fingers still shook so violently that her attempts to shed herself of the thin, clingy fabric were clumsy.

But then she was standing there, bare and quaking.

He was silent for so long that she thought she might be sick.

"Madeline." Finally, he growled her name and crossed to where she stood in two quick strides. And then she was in his arms. His grip was rough, his kiss harsh. But having his arms around her helped to quell the worst of her fear.

This was William.

This was her husband.

She was safe.

It was only when his hands came to her bared breasts that she flinched and pulled away before she could stop herself.

He froze. "Did I hurt you?"

She shook her head. "No, it's just…"

It's just my mother tried to sell me, you see. It's only that I was mishandled by a handful of men. I cannot forget the way it felt to have strangers touching me.

No words came out. How was one supposed to say something like that? And to a man who believed her to be pure and chaste.

You are *pure.*

Are you? It was Foley's voice in her head. It was his smug sneer she saw in her mind's eye.

"Is it me then?" William's voice was harsh as he stepped away from her. Picking up her night-rail, he tossed it to her. "Is it only my touch that is so abhorrent to you?"

She blinked in surprise at the icy tinge to his voice, the way his eyes snapped with anger.

Her lips parted, but she didn't speak quickly enough. And then he was stalking past her to the bed, where he'd been sitting. "No need to lie any longer, love."

Her insides tumbled and churned at the snide way he used the endearment. That connection she'd felt between them, the bond they'd been slowly and sweetly forming…

It seemed to snap in a heartbeat.

"I-I'm not lying," she said.

He threw a piece of paper at her. "Then what's this?"

She blinked down at the crumpled paper. And for a moment, she was too confused to understand. But as she reached for it, she recognized it—and her heart slammed into her throat.

"Who were you writing to? Who do you expect to come and save you? Some lover?" William paced in front of her. She could all but feel the anger and tension rippling off of him, and it terrified her.

"My brother," she whispered.

"What?" he snapped.

She stood slowly, wrapping the fabric around her. Never in her life had she felt more vulnerable and exposed than she did right now. In front of her own husband. But the way he was looking at her…

His look was that of a stranger. His warm eyes were cold and shuttered. His voice was barely recognizable. Where was the loveable drunk who'd stumbled into her room, or the chivalrous knight who'd stolen her from her cruel family? Where was the gentle, patient, loving husband who'd been so heartachingly respectful this past fortnight?

"M-my brother," she repeated, her voice shaking along with her legs. "The letter was for him."

He stopped pacing. "Your brother."

"Yes."

"Viscount Marlow," he said.

"Yes, my—William." *Oh, blast.* Tears were threatening, and she'd very nearly called him "my lord." But he did not seem to like her William now. He looked like a stranger.

The silence that followed felt like it might crush her, but she could not lift her head to face him. Until at last, he spoke again.

"Did you mean it?"

Then her head came up and her gaze darted to his. The pain she'd heard in his tone lanced her heart as surely as a sword. "My lord?"

"The note," he gritted out with impatience. "Did you mean it? Are you really so very unhappy here with me—"

"No," she said quickly.

He leveled her with a glare. "Then why did you write it?"

"I didn't."

Rage contorted his handsome features, and when he strode toward her again, she flinched. But he did not strike her. Of course not. He was not mad like her father nor cruel like her mother. He was…hurt.

Her lungs faltered at the sight of his pain.

"Do not lie to me, Madeline," he said.

"I'm not lying."

"You expect me to believe that this was not your note?"

She shook her head, her tongue tied in knots. "No. Yes. I mean, it was from me, but I did not write it." She met his gaze. "I cannot write. Nor read."

His chin jerked back as if this startled him. Shame had heat creeping into her cheeks. "My father believes it dangerous to teach women to write. My brother tried to teach me, but he was caught and beaten and—"

His firm grip on her shoulders had her stopping short.

"Madeline, are you truly unhappy here with me?"

The pleading look behind that mask of anger made her heart feel like it was splitting in two.

She'd hurt him.

She'd hurt this man who'd been so very dear.

She shook her head, the words finally tumbling out of her mouth. "No, you don't understand. I had someone write that for me when I was staying with Lord and Lady Fallenmore. Before we wed."

His brows drew down, his gaze darting back and forth between her eyes like he could read all her secrets. "Why?"

"Because I was afraid," she said. "You seemed kind, but I was afraid when we were alone together..." Her breath hitched on a sob. It seemed ridiculous now to even think that this man would hurt her. "I was afraid I would be trapped here."

"With me."

"Yes. But..." She sniffed, her voice pleading. "That was before, and I...I don't want to leave. I never want to leave you."

She saw a crack in that cold, hard armor he wore so well. "You don't?"

"I don't. Truthfully, I forgot it was in there. I'd had that doctor write it for me just in case...I wanted to know that someone would come to save me if you...if you..."

"If I turned out to be like your father?"

"Yes." She wrapped her arms around her waist. "I'm sorry, William. I should have destroyed it that very first night. You've been so kind to me, and I am so sorry—"

"No." All at once, his coldness crumpled, and he pulled her into his chest, burying his face in her wet hair. "No, love. I am sorry. I should have just asked. I should have known there'd be an explanation."

She gripped his face and brought his lips down to hers in a messy, frantic kiss that left her trembling in an altogether different sort of way.

"You are mine," he whispered harshly between kisses.

"Yes."

His lips were on her cheeks, her forehead, her neck, her shoulders. When he tugged the fabric away from her wet skin, she let him. This time she did not try to shield herself, and when his palms skimmed over her breasts, so gently, she arched into him.

"I want you to touch me," she whispered. "All of me."

I want you to make me forget.

She swallowed those words. But that was what she wanted, and she tried to show him with every eager kiss and every touch. "Make me yours completely," she said. "I want this. I want...I want you."

He groaned and then bent down to lift her into his arms. "My sweet little love."

He set her down gently, and with his every breath, he seemed to drink in more of her. His gaze took her in and despite her nerves, she refused to flinch away from his touch.

When his hand came down on her upper thigh, her hips arched up to meet him.

He chuckled. "So responsive, my sweet."

Will she be a frigid little thing?

Who cares? The man with the beard had said, his gaze holding hers as he'd laughed. *It's all the better when they try to fight you off.*

Oh, aye, his friend had laughed. *Percer here likes to break 'em. You like to hear 'em beg, don't you, you old dog?*

She squeezed her eyes shut as if that could make the voices go away.

"No, my sweet." Hayden's fingers were gentle on her chin, his wrist brushed against her neck so her pulse pounded against his. "Don't close your eyes. You have nothing to fear from me."

She tried to nod, but that flash of memory had left her queasy.

"Make me forget." The words slipped out before she could stop them.

His brows drew together. "Forget what, love?"

She didn't answer, but she saw him leap to the wrong conclusion. Guilt clouded his gaze. "My anger just now. Is that what you mean?" He muttered a curse aimed at himself. "I'm sorry if I scared you. I should know better. Your father… He was violent, wasn't he?"

She nodded.

"Mine was, too."

She blinked, taken aback by the admission as much as by the haunted look in his eyes.

"I would never hurt you like that. I would never—"

"I know."

He looked like he might continue to argue the point, but he looked into her eyes and nodded. "I suppose I ought to explain my…" he swallowed thickly, "my reaction before."

She waited, her breath sounding too loud to her own ears.

"My father was mean," he said simply. "And my mother could not bear it. She took a lover. I'd like to imagine it was someone kind to her. I hope she'd had that, for a little while at least."

She lifted her hands, settling them on his shoulders. "And then?"

"My father found out. Murdered them both."

She gasped. "Oh, William—"

He leaned down and kissed her. "It's all right. It was a long time ago. But then he remarried, and the woman was…well, she was a harlot. There's no other way to put it."

This time her eyes widened in shock. She'd never heard him sound so cold and disdainful, not even when he'd thought she'd betrayed him. "H-how so?"

"She was power hungry. More beautiful than you could imagine…and the most clever actress I've ever met. She had my father convinced that she was an innocent. Flirtatious and charming, but the very picture of demurity and piety around him."

She swallowed hard, waiting for the next blow.

"But it was all a lie. I caught her making a cuckold of him. She knew he'd believe me over her, and so she set me up."

"How?"

"She came into my rooms. Seduced me. I was still young, just barely a man. My body responded to her quickly, and…" He winced as he eyed her horrified expression. "Well, one moment I was asleep, the next I was tupping my stepmother. And she made sure we were caught."

Madeline gasped.

"Not by my father, but by one of the servants. She paid them off, but she had her insurance. If it was ever her word against mine, she would win."

"Oh, William, that's…that's awful."

His smile was wry. "Not a pretty story, is it? But I thought you deserved to know. I don't find it easy to trust. Especially women. And…" He pulled his head back so his gaze could meet hers. "I cannot share."

The ferocity in his voice had her heart leaping.

He leaned down closer so he could read every emotion in her eyes. "Do you understand me, love? I will not have any other man touching you or looking upon you or…" He eased back. "I am not violent. I will never hurt you. But you should know here and now that I am not capable of forgiveness either. Not when it comes to a betrayal of vows or a breach of trust."

She stared at him with wide eyes. That awful memory reared its ugly head, and for a moment it almost came tumbling out. The whole sordid tale. But she couldn't do it. There was no way she'd risk seeing disgust in his eyes, not now when he was finally opening to her completely.

This was the man she'd wed. Complicated, tarnished…but hers.

"I won't share you either," she said instead. It was the only other truth she knew for certain. He was hers, just as she was his.

This made him smile. "No?"

She shook her head, her arms wrapping around his shoulders

tightly. "I don't want to share you either."

He pressed his lips to her ear and took a long, shuddering breath. "Then you shan't, love. I am all yours. And you are all mine."

She squeezed her eyes shut. The words were as good as a vow. Better than the vow they'd made before their friends and the parson. This was a new commitment, and one she would not risk by exposing her own dark deeds.

He kissed her hard, and then he was shedding his shirt and leaning down over her until his hard chest brushed against her nipples.

She gasped at the sudden rush of sensation.

"Thank you for sharing your body with me," he said. "I will cherish it. I will cherish you."

"Ch-cherish?" she managed as his lips trailed over the top of her breasts.

"Mmm," he growled, his gaze darting up, mischievous and playful as he took the hard nipple between his lips.

"Oh!" She squirmed at the sweet sensation, wriggling wildly at the influx of heat and tension. His warm breath on that sensitive nub made her shiver. And then his tongue lapped at the hardened peak as his devilish gaze lifted up to meet hers. "That's…that's…"

"That's just the beginning, love," he warned. "If I scare you, tell me, yes?"

She nodded. "But you won't."

"You sound so sure."

She smiled, his lips on her skin seemed to be branding her as his, removing all trace of anyone else's grasping hands. "I am sure."

His grin was wolfish, and it made her insides clench. "Now, let me explore this delicious body of yours." He growled his approval as he licked and nipped at the undersides of her breasts and then lower, taking his sweet time as he worked his way over her ribs and belly.

The scrape of stubble against her too-sensitive skin was a

sweet torment as his tongue flicked out to taste her skin, dropping chaste little kisses along her ribs before tickling her belly with a nuzzling kiss that made her giggle even as she gasped for air.

All the while, he made his way lower, taking his time as he did as he'd promised. He cherished every last inch of her.

Her breath was coming in pants, and her fingers were buried in his hair when he stopped at the dark thatch of curls between her thighs. He lifted his head. "I love this sweet little marker," he said, a grin on his lips as he pressed an open-mouthed kiss to the small birthmark at the top of her right thigh. "This is mine," he whispered, his hot breath against her curls bringing a jab of longing.

Her hips couldn't stay still. There was a yearning sensation inside her that made her feel needier than she'd ever known. She ached to be closer, to feel fuller.

"Please, William," she whimpered.

"Please what, love?" he teased, his nose and lips nuzzling at the soft skin of her inner thighs. "What is it you want, wife?"

She didn't know. But her body ached with wanting, her hips arching off the bed as she silently begged for more.

"Mmm, more for me, eh?" he teased as he caught hold of her bottom, his fingers gripping the soft flesh of her cheeks as he lifted her hips higher, forcing her thighs further apart.

For a long moment, he lay there with his face buried between her thighs. His breath was ragged and hot against her *mons*. He nuzzled her there with a growl that sent hot shivers down her legs and to her toes.

"William," she pleaded.

His tongue flicked out suddenly, darting out to part her folds with a firm stroke that made her cry out. "Yes, love?" he asked, wicked amusement in his voice at the way she was coming apart in his arms.

Her head rolled from side to side as she wiggled beneath the hot torture of his breath.

"Please." She tugged on his hair, trying to pull him up so he might thrust himself inside of her and relieve this ache. Her inner muscles were still clenching, desperate for the feel of him.

His low chuckle sent goosebumps over her skin.

"Greedy little kitten." And then he kissed her.

Down there.

His mouth open, he kissed her parted folds with the same sort of wet, hot, messy fervor that he kissed her mouth. Her head fell back, and her body arched as pleasure speared through her at the odd and exquisite sensation of his tongue and his lips moving over her womanhood.

"William!"

"I've got you, love," he said as he continued to worship her sex. "This is mine, isn't it?" He thrust his tongue inside of her, and she screamed her response.

"Yes!"

He kissed the hard nub at the apex of her folds in satisfaction. "Good girl. Say it for me."

She forgot all modesty as need swept through her. Her fingers gripped his head, holding him closer.

"It's yours," she panted. "I'm yours. My body is all yours."

He lifted his head to smile at her. "That's right, love. And don't you ever forget."

He buried his face between her thighs once more, and this time he thrust two fingers deep inside her as he ravished her quim. His fingers thrust again and again as she writhed.

He didn't stop until her body shook from her release. And when she came back to earth, her legs still trembling, she realized he'd done it.

He'd made her forget.

For a little while, at least, he'd purged her body and her mind of those nasty, haunting images. And as he slid up beside her and pulled her into his arms, she knew she'd meant every word of her vow.

Her body was his and his alone.

From now until forever.

CHAPTER THIRTEEN

W ILLIAM WAS HOLDING her hands. "Yes, but are you sure you're up for it?"

She smiled. "You said so yourself. At some point, I must interact with high society."

"Yes, but…a ball?"

He looked so horrified that all of his friends broke out laughing.

"It won't be so bad, Hayden," Philippa said.

Benedict's arched brow as he looked to his wife said that he begged to differ. "It's a ball, Philippa. By its very nature, it must be bad."

"Tedious and dull, perhaps," Raff said. "But not so very dreadful."

"Mmm." Evangeline looked as though she was considering the matter. "I'm with Hayden. I still do not enjoy these large balls."

Raff wrapped his arms around his wife. As it was just the six of them at the picnic, all rules of society had broken down entirely, with displays of affection going utterly unchecked. Not that Madeline minded. She'd been enjoying this day immensely. And the fact that the outing had been William's plan and meant for her…

She squeezed his hand as she stole a glance at the man who'd stolen her heart. She'd felt closer than ever with him this last week. She'd not seen nor heard from that vile Foley again, and when surrounded by her doting husband and her newfound, powerful friends…

It was almost too easy to forget about his threats. After all, none of her new acquaintances liked the man, and her mother had long since distanced herself from society.

She tilted her head back so she could soak in the spring sunshine on this gorgeous day.

If only she knew where her brother was at this moment. If she could only get word to him, she'd say her life was perfect.

"Happy, love?" William's voice was low next to her ear.

She turned her smile in his direction. "Very. And you?"

"Perfect." He leaned in closer until his lips grazed her ear. "I had an idea for what we might do later, once we are alone."

She couldn't squelch the giggle before it escaped.

He pulled back with a look of fake admonishment. "My goodness, where did your mind go?" He tsked. "Naughty girl."

She laughed harder. "Was that not what you meant?"

He dropped his voice lower, his gaze filled with promise. "That is always on my agenda."

She fell against him as she laughed, and he wrapped an arm around her shoulders as he continued, his voice filled with amusement. "But, at this particular moment, I was actually referring to something else."

She pulled back to look at him. "What is it?"

"Well, I thought…" He shifted, looking adorably hesitant. "I thought perhaps I might begin teaching you how to read and write." He cleared his throat when she continued to gape at him in silence. "If you would like."

A wave of emotion had her throwing her arms around him and squeezing him tight, heedless of the others who were busy talking and laughing amongst themselves.

He ran a hand over her back. "Is that a yes?"

She nodded, her throat too choked to speak. "Yes. Definitely yes."

"Good, because…" He met her gaze when she drew back. "I would not like for you to feel beholden to me or anyone else. If you wish to send letters to your brother or learn about a topic on your own…" His brows drew down. "I want you to have your freedom. You know that, don't you?"

She nodded quickly. "I do know that." She touched his cheek. "And I love that about you. About…us."

He smiled and captured her hand to kiss it. "Good. Then tonight, yes?"

"Tonight," she agreed with a nod. "Yes."

But when they returned back to their townhome, their plans were altered thanks to a visitor.

"Lady Ashburn is here to see you, my lady," the butler informed her.

Madeline froze as William hovered beside her. "Your mother? What does she want?"

Her pulse sounded too loud as her blood rushed past her ears. The countess rarely left their estate, so why now? Why here?

William started toward the drawing room, but Madeline stopped him. "No. Please. She's here to see me. Let me speak with her."

He stared at her with questions in his eyes.

What *did* she want?

There was only one way to find out.

Squaring her shoulders, she took a deep breath, only then realizing she was squeezing William's hand much too hard.

"Are you all right?" he asked.

"Yes. Just…surprised, that's all."

"Let me come with you," he said.

She shook her head; fears were spiking left and right. She didn't know what her mother might say or do, but she was quite certain that she didn't want William to be any part of it.

"This is my home now," she said with a smile she didn't truly feel. "She cannot hurt me here."

He considered her carefully. "If you're certain…"

She nodded. "I am."

"I'll be close," he said. "Just say the word, and I will be there."

"I know," she whispered.

With one last squeeze of his hand, she left him. Her mother was standing, and in this different setting, Madeline was certain she looked…smaller. Frailer.

But when the older woman turned to face her, Madeline knew she was no less terrifying.

There was no spark of humanity in her eyes as she smiled her greeting. "Ah, at last. You know I don't like to be kept waiting."

"I did not know you were here—"

"No matter. You're here now, so let us get the business done so I might be on my way." Her lips curled in a sneer. "I have no desire to exchange pleasantries with a weak little bastard child."

"Then what are you doing here?" Madeline took some pride in the fact that her voice was smooth and even, no hint of her fear seeping through.

"I'm here for the money, of course." Her smile was nasty as she moved closer. "I'm sure Foley spoke to you on my behalf. But he tells me he was unable to give you the details of our new arrangement."

"What new arrangement?" she snapped. "We have no arrangement."

"Don't we?" The countess's smile fell. "You cheated me out of my fortune, you little brat. First your father squandered the estate and then you robbed me of my one chance to have a tidy sum of my own."

"I didn't—"

"You think I don't want to escape that hell, too?"

Madeline stumbled back a step. The older woman's eyes were wide and…crazed.

Good Lord, was there something in the water at their estate? Or had her father been drawn to someone similar to himself?

Madeline shook her head. This was not the time to sort it out.

"I owe you nothing. You were going to sell me—"

"Yes, and instead, I got a third of what I could have made from Mr. Percer. How did you manage it, child? Hmm?"

"I didn't rob or cheat," Madeline protested. "I was never yours to sell."

"Hush, you little whore," her mother said. "I have plenty of witnesses who will swear to the fact that we locked you away to keep you from harming yourself with your loose morals and your salacious ways."

"No one will believe that."

"Won't they?" The countess's brows arched. "What about your husband? You don't think he'll look at you differently if he were to learn that he'd been tricked into marrying a slattern?"

"That's not true."

The countess shocked her with a laugh. "Oh, stupid little child. Still so naive. It doesn't matter what's true, only what one believes."

"He won't believe you," she said. As she said it, she heard his voice. The pained look when he'd told her he'd never forgive her if she were with another.

He'd believe her side of the story...wouldn't he?

But even if he did, would he look at her differently? Would this newfound love be tainted?

The countess chuckled. "You witless cow. Still so very easy to read, you know that, yes? You don't trust that he'll believe you, and you shouldn't. Men are so easy to sway. Just prey on their weakness and probe their fears..." She waved a hand. "So very easy to manipulate."

"What do you want?"

The countess smiled. "The money you owe me, of course."

"I don't have money—"

"But your husband does." She moved closer. "One thousand pounds—"

Madeline gasped at the outrageous amount.

"Oh, not all at once. You can pay me over time, if you so

choose."

"But I don't…I can't…"

"You can. It's simple, dear. You ask for a little pin money here, an additional allowance for a new gown there. It couldn't be simpler."

"But I—"

"Foley will be at the ball tomorrow night. I heard you will be making your grand entrance." Her smile was pure bitterness. "How lovely for you. It would be such a shame if your big night were to be ruined by a row. Or worse, rampant rumors about your shameful acts."

"You wouldn't—"

"I would, and you know it," the countess cut in with a voice so sharp it made Madeline flinch. "I despise you and I always have. Having to raise some poor country lass's babe. Let everyone think you were mine? The indignity, child. You have no idea."

Madeline gaped. Her mother had always been cold. Cruel and sometimes violent. But she'd never heard this rage from her. Like a lifetime of anger was trying to climb out of her.

"The only use you were to me was as a means to a fortune. Truth be told, I was looking forward to watching you break. To see you reduced to a life as some man's whore. And in return, I'd have made a fortune." She shook her head with a tsk. "But you couldn't even do that right." She headed toward the door. "So, no, Madeline. Do not doubt that I would ruin your new life. And happily." She paused to look back. "Just give me a reason, child. Any reason will do."

CHAPTER FOURTEEN

MADELINE HAD BEEN acting oddly all night. All day, too. Truly, she'd been behaving erratically ever since her mother came to visit. But she'd shut down his every attempt to find out what that wicked woman had wanted.

"Nervous, sweetheart?" he asked as the carriage slowed to a crawl behind the other coaches arriving at the townhome where the ball was to be held.

"I suppose I am," she said, her smile weak.

"We can turn back," he offered.

"No." She shook her head quickly. "I must face this sooner or later, mustn't I?"

He watched her for a long moment. Somehow, he didn't believe she merely meant facing the *ton*. Her chin was set in such a way that it looked like she was about to head into battle.

He reached for her hand and tugged until she was nestled against his side. "There now, that's better."

She laughed even as she burrowed into his chest. "We've nearly arrived. Now is hardly the time for us to be caught doing something improper in the carriage."

He grinned as he tilted her head up for a long, lingering kiss. "Tell me, wife, is this so very improper?"

"No, I suppose not," she said breathlessly when he pulled away.

"Hmm, and this?" He dipped his head to kiss her neck, careful not to muss her coif.

"I...I don't think so," she breathed.

He grinned before nipping at her neck. This was better. Much better. A breathless, dazed Madeline was far superior to the anxious, fidgety lady she'd been just a moment before. He despised seeing her on edge like that. But fortunately, he knew exactly how to relax her tense muscles.

"Now, my dear," he continued, his hungry gaze taking in the way her nipples were jutting out against the fabric of her bodice. "It's clear to me what you need."

"Is it?" Her eyes were dazed as he trailed his fingers over those hard tips making her shiver. She pressed one perfectly rounded tit into his palm, silently begging for more. But a second later, she recoiled. "Wait, we mustn't."

He pushed the curtain aside to peer out. "We still have plenty of time."

"Oh, but...oh!" She squeaked in surprise when he pulled her onto his lap, her back to his chest and her legs straddling his thighs.

"Too many bloody clothes," he muttered against her neck as he went about hitching up her gown.

"But we can't," she said.

Her protests would have been more effective if she wasn't pressing her bottom against his erection, wiggling and shifting like a wanton mistress.

He grinned as he bit the soft skin at the bottom of her neck, just hard enough to make her gasp. "No more of that, my sweet. You'll have me losing control before I'm inside you."

She whimpered but kept her hips still as he released his shaft from his trousers and found the slit in her undergarments. It prodded against her backside, rigid and throbbing, ready to be encased in her tight heat.

She moaned when his fingers slid inside to touch her wet, slick heat.

"You're drenched for me, darling." He slid his free hand up to the edge of her bodice, tugging until her breasts spilled over. Her hips ground back.

"Uh uh," he said with a tsk as he pinched a nipple hard in admonishment. "You do as you're told, my sweet."

Her back arched, and he rewarded her with another hard pinch that made her gasp.

"That's right. You're mine to command tonight, aren't you, darling?"

"Oh, yes. I'm all yours."

He squeezed her tit as he pressed his erection up against her, loving the way her breath grew rapid and ragged.

He slid his other hand around, just beneath her skirts to cup her sex. Oh hell, she was so wet for him, he had to clench his jaw to keep from tossing her on her knees and thrusting into her from behind.

"Tell me, wife, do you enjoy knowing we could be caught?" he whispered in her ear.

Her moan was answer enough, but he used his knees to pry her thighs wider apart and gave her quim a light spank that had her whimpering with need.

"Say it aloud," he commanded, his voice low in her ear. "You like it, don't you, my naughty girl?"

He already knew she did. And he liked it, too. The danger of being caught made his every sense heightened.

"I...I..." She shuddered in his arms when his palm pressed firmly to her heat.

"Tell me the truth," he whispered. "Tell your husband just how naughty you are. Does it give you a thrill knowing that at any moment we could stop. That the high and mighty of society could hear you being fucked in a coach?"

"Yes," she hissed.

"Good," he said. "Because I am your husband, so there is no shame here. No guilt. Do you understand?"

She nodded.

"Only pleasure," he said. "And you can be as wicked as you want with me, can't you?"

"Yes, William," she whimpered as his fingers slid inside her drawers to play with her slick folds.

She turned her head, and he claimed her mouth in a hot, open kiss that made her moan.

They had to be quick, but he'd make sure it was filled with pleasure.

"Such a sweet little wife," he said. "But I love that you're naughty for me."

"Yes, you," she whimpered as his fingers pinched her nipple again, hard enough to make her gasp. "Only you."

"Good girl," he praised, satisfaction clear in his voice as he nipped at the bottom of her ear.

He'd discovered that nothing made him harder than when she pledged herself to him and him alone. Even now, he swelled against her, his bollocks so tight and hard he was blinded with lust.

"Will you scream, my sweet wife?" he whispered. "Will you scream my name so every lord and dandy knows that you are mine to bed whenever I wish?"

She moaned and trembled, his words making her writhe in his arms. "If you want me to," she said.

He grinned against her neck. "Such an obedient bride."

He gave her quim another light slap as he spread her thighs even further. They both looked down, and he groaned as she whimpered at the sight of her wet cunny on full display as his hand gave another smack.

"You like the sting of it, don't you?" He barely recognized his own voice.

They'd been exploring new boundaries every day and every night, but here in the dark, secretive, forbidden setting, they were both discovering something new.

"Do you like it?" he asked. For a moment, he stilled. Her body was reacting to his harsh touch, but until she said so, he forced himself to stay still.

She placed one of her hands over his and ground his palm into her sex. "I love it," she panted. "I want more."

He smiled against her neck before lapping at her skin. "When we get home, I'll give you a proper spanking, hmm?"

Her breath came in shallow gasps, and he knew she was imagining it, too. "Yes," she breathed. "Yes, please."

"Tell me what you need from your husband," he commanded.

"I need you inside me," she said.

He sucked on her earlobe. "How do you want it?"

"Hard," she said. "I want you to take me hard."

"Good girl," he growled.

Her whimpers grew high and needy as he adjusted his hard length and lifted her slightly. Then he tugged on her hips and thrust up inside her with a rough shove that had them both groaning in pleasure.

"Do you like sitting on my cock, love?" he teased as he forced himself to stay still.

"I love it," she breathed, her hips moving as she tried to find satisfaction. He helped her to bounce up and down a few times, giving them both a taste of the pleasure to come.

"Touch your tits, love," he growled into her ear.

He dipped his head over her shoulder to watch, and his sweet wife didn't waste a second. She teased her nipples and fondled her breasts with abandon, showing him exactly the way she liked to be touched as he looked on.

The carriage rattled as they moved again, and he felt her tense. "We're almost there," she whispered, reality returning as her hands froze over her nipples.

His fingers bit into her thighs. "You're not going anywhere until you find pleasure, do you understand? I don't care if the door is thrown open and all of Mayfair sees me tupping my wife."

He growled in her ear. "You will ride my cock until you come. Is that understood?"

Her breath caught at his commanding tone, and then something seemed to shift in her, just like it did when they were alone in bed and he took control. He could all but see her relinquish her fears as she gave herself up to his commands.

"Yes, William," she whispered as she rocked her hips vigorously. He gripped her thighs to help her find purchase and soon his sweet little wife was riding him with hard thrusts that had them both panting as he hardened even further inside her.

The carriage rattled again, and the driver called out for the horses to stop.

He moved his hand to her cunny, fingering that hard, sensitive nub. "Now, love," he gritted out. "Come for me now."

She came with a muffled cry.

She was already readjusting her bodice by the time he was through, and he helped her to slide off of him and right her gown.

"I'll be a mess," she said, though she still wore a satisfied grin that made his heart slam erratically against its cage.

"Your gown and your hair are still perfect," he assured her. "But if you mean you'll have my seed spilling down your thighs all evening…" He leaned over to kiss her blush with a grin. "I must admit, I love that."

"You would," she muttered, but her look of disapproval was ruined by the laughter in her eyes.

"All night I'll be imagining when I can do it again. Where I can take you…"

She pursed her lips. "Are you trying to scandalize me, husband?"

"That depends." He gripped her hand and brought it to his lips. "Is it working?"

Her answering giggle made his heart trip.

Then they arrived, and the carriage door was thrown open. If anyone wondered why his wife's cheeks were such a vivid red, no one asked.

And then they were in the midst of a crush entering the already crowded ballroom.

"You're certain you're up for this," he said to Madeline.

She smiled sweetly and squeezed his arm. "No. But I have to do this." She drew in a deep breath. "I must."

He leaned down because the closer they drew to the ballroom where musicians played, the harder it was to hear and be heard. "Only say the word, my darling, and we will leave. You have nothing to prove to me."

She shot him a wry smile. "No, only to all the rest of society."

He chuckled. "Who cares what they think?"

She arched a brow. "Don't you?"

He laughed outright then. "My dear, you do know I spent the better part of my adulthood attempting to scandalize this lot, don't you?"

She arched a brow, and for a moment, he was certain the rest of this crowd ceased to exist. "Is that why you proposed?"

He leaned in closer. "I proposed because I was caught in your room alone. I married you because you were the sweetest little creature I'd ever met. But I'm bringing you here tonight to show you off because marrying you was the smartest thing I have ever done."

She arched her brows in disbelief, and he knew she was thinking of the night they first met. "The smartest, hmm?"

He leaned in so only she could hear. "Let every other man here weep for not having had the good sense to climb that ghastly tower wall before I did."

She burst out laughing at his teasing, and the sound made his heart warm. The sound was better than any music. And that light in her eyes was so genuine and so pure, it humbled him.

"Now, now, Hayden," Philippa's voice cut into the moment, and he backed away from his wife to see that Benedict and Philippa were on her other side. "I hope you don't mean to keep your darling bride all to yourself tonight."

Malcolm and Vivian joined them, and Vivian greeted Madeline with a warm embrace. "I've been meaning to check in on you this week to see how you're adjusting."

"I'm not *that* difficult to live with," Hayden joked.

"Aren't you?" Raff and Evangeline joined them as well. "Don't tell me you've gone and matured on us, Hayden, old friend."

His friends laughed as he pretended to be horrified. "I wouldn't dream of it."

Madeline grinned up at him. "I hear so many stories about your reckless behavior and yet you've always been so honorable and upstanding with me."

Malcolm cleared his throat. "Have you forgotten the state he was in the night you first met?"

Madeline laughed. "No, indeed. But he sobered up quite quickly when he realized he was forced to marry me."

Hayden smiled down at her. "I'd do it all over again, any day."

Her eyes were so soft with affection, he nearly missed the glint of wariness and regret that flickered in her gaze before she quickly looked away.

He placed a hand on her back, that earlier nagging sensation back. She'd been on edge today. But he did not think it was merely nerves over her first ball.

Especially not now when she was surrounded by friends.

"Come, Madeline," Philippa said, holding out her arm. "Let us ladies show you about the room."

Vivian and Evangeline followed Phillipa, laughing.

"She just wants to fill you in on the latest gossip," Vivian said.

Evangeline glanced back at him. "Don't worry, Hayden, we'll bring her back to you soon enough."

He smiled as they walked away, but he felt a knot of tension forming with each step she took away from him.

Raff clapped a hand on his shoulder. "You can't keep her at your side every moment of every day. Trust me, I've tried."

Hayden laughed.

"He's right," Malcolm said. "Madeline has come a long way since that first night you rescued her, but at some point, you'll have to trust her to stand on her own."

Trust. That work rankled. He *did* trust her. Though that night when he'd read her note to her brother…

Well, he wasn't proud of where his thoughts had gone. Nor how quickly.

"How do you trust someone when you've really only just met?" The words tumbled out of him before he'd even decided to talk.

To his surprise, it was the normally quiet and gruff Benedict who responded. "You make the choice to trust, and time will tell if you're right or wrong."

Hayden stared at his wife's receding figure as she was swallowed up in the crowd. Was it really as simple as that? Choosing to trust. Was that what it came down to?

"Madeline hasn't given you any reason to believe she's not trustworthy, has she?" Raff asked with concern.

"No," he said quickly. "No, of course not."

Malcolm watched him quietly. They'd all known him for an age, but it was Malcolm who'd been there during the worst days of his stepmother's brief reign in his father's household. He suspected Malcolm understood more of what he was feeling than anyone.

But his stepmother's actions were best forgotten, just like he'd all but forgotten the woman herself when he'd sent her off to the continent after his father died.

His wife wasn't anything like her.

"What's *he* doing here?" Benedict growled.

Hayden didn't even bother to look. That was the question they all raised whenever that lowlife Foley arrived. Raff suspected the man was blackmailing and exploiting his way into society, as no one seemed to enjoy his company.

Well, no one except for Madeline's mother.

"And what's he doing talking to Hayden's wife?" Raff added.

That had Hayden turning to stare. Though there wasn't much to see. Madeline and Foley had a brief exchange and then she was back to taking a turn with her friends around the dancefloor.

It was over in an instant, but Hayden found himself stewing over it for an age.

"Honestly, how has that man not been killed yet?" he finally spit out.

Benedict arched a brow. "I assume you mean Foley." He nodded as he thought it over. "Valid question.

Raff scowled. "I should have done it when I had the chance."

"And I," Benedict added.

Malcolm was eyeing the weasel thoughtfully. "From what we know of him, I'd guess he holds too much power over the wrong people." He eyed Hayden thoughtfully. "Don't you think?"

Hayden stiffened. Foley had been there with the countess on the night he'd arrived in her room. He clearly had some interest in Madeline's family, and he knew far too much about the circumstances behind his and Madeline's marriage.

That was enough to have him stop Foley when he passed. "What did you want with my wife?"

"Pardon?" Foley's feigned confusion as he glanced around him at the curious onlookers passing them only made Hayden's anger grow.

"What did you want with her?" he repeated through a tight jaw.

"I'm afraid you're mistaken, my lord," he said in that ingratiating tone of his that never failed to rankle.

"I saw you talking to her." Hayden leaned in close so only Foley could hear. "If you have any sense of self-preservation you'll stay far away from Madeline."

Foley laughed. "Oh, my lord, you misunderstand. I do not deny that we spoke, but it was she who asked to speak to me."

Hayden glared. "She would never seek out the likes of you."

Foley smiled, and the smile made Hayden's gut twist with apprehension. "Apologies, my lord. But it is rather amusing the way you have bought her little act." He held his hands up to his cheeks, his eyes wide with feigned innocence. "Oh, poor me. Such an innocent, helpless creature."

Hayden snagged Foley's cravat and gripped it tight.

"Not here," Raff said, a hand on his shoulder. His friends crowded behind him, and Hayden let go with an oath.

"You dare to speak ill of my wife?"

"Oh, no, no, my lord. Once again, you misunderstand. You see, I find her to be quite delightful. I admire her theatrical skills immensely."

Hayden growled, and Benedict stepped between them. "I'd leave now, Foley, before a challenge is issued and your life comes to an abrupt end."

Foley paled at that, but he sneered at Hayden. "Don't say I didn't warn you."

Hayden snarled, a fist forming before Malcolm caught his arm.

Foley was backing away. "I'd check my pockets if I were you. The mad earl's daughter has a light touch…"

"Why you—"

"But if you really want to know the truth about your wife…" Foley smiled when he realized all four men were listening. "Head to the gaming hell on Vestry Lane. Ask for Mr. Percer. He'll tell you what she's really about."

Foley turned and disappeared.

"Don't listen to him," Malcolm said in a low voice. "He's just trying to rattle you."

And he'd succeeded.

Hayden's gut churned. He wanted to trust his wife. He wanted to laugh off Foley's veiled words and that ominous warning. "To what end?" he muttered aloud. "What is his game?"

Philippa was the first of the ladies to rejoin them a short while later, and Hayden took her aside.

"Philippa, did Foley approach Madeline? Or did my wife seek him out?"

She blinked in surprise but then her brows came down in

thought. "She sought him out, I believe. She said something about having him pass along a message to her mother." She paled. "Did I do wrong in letting her talk to him? I should have known better than to let her so much as go near that poor excuse for a man."

"No, no," he rushed to reassure her. "He is a friend to her mother, I just…I just wanted to be sure he wasn't preying on her."

She nodded. She'd been one of the ladies the louse had preyed upon, so Hayden supposed Philippa understood better than anyone.

He turned back to see Madeline laughing at something Vivian said.

The trouble was, he wasn't entirely certain if Madeline was the prey. Why had she sought him out?

He tried to swipe the thought aside, but his gut coiled with anger, the whiff of betrayal getting stronger with her every nervous glance and shuttered gaze.

Could there possibly be any truth to what Foley had said?

No.

Never.

But then again…he had to be certain.

CHAPTER FIFTEEN

MADELINE WATCHED WILLIAM the whole way home.
Or rather, she stared at his profile. He never once glanced her way. And he was silent for the entire ride, not even responding to her questions about how he'd enjoyed his evening.

At first, she'd thought it was her own guilt making her paranoid. She'd been so desperate to stop her stepmother from going through with her horrid threats that she'd done something so shameful, she'd barely been able to look her husband in the eyes earlier today.

She'd asked him for pin money like the countess had said. But it hadn't been enough. Not nearly. And then she'd seen money on his desk. Funds set aside for household items.

Her mouth was dry and her stomach queasy at the memory of it. So quick. So easy. She'd had the money in her reticule in seconds.

Did he know? Was that why he was avoiding looking at her?

She pressed her shaking hands to her belly, but her chest was tight with fear as they rode in silence.

By the time they arrived home and were heading up the stairs to her bedroom, her belly was a knotted mess of worry.

"William," she started.

She stopped when he gave her a warning look, glancing at the maid who curtsied as they passed.

Not in front of the servants, his glare said.

Her mouth went dry. When they entered her bedroom, he shut the door with an ominous snick.

"W-william?" she said, her palms growing clammy when he turned to face her.

This…this wasn't William. The man before her might as well have been a stranger. The warmth in his gaze had gone cold, and the smile on his lips was nowhere to be seen.

"William, is something wrong? Have I… Have I done something wrong?"

Her guilty conscience reared up at that.

Have you done something wrong? Aside from lie and steal and betray your husband's trust?

He watched her for a long moment, and she clasped her hands tight when she realized…he knew her. He always saw straight through her. And right now, what he saw made her want to weep.

"Did you do something wrong," he finally said, drawing out the words like he was mulling them over. "I don't know, Madeline. Why don't you tell me? Have you done something wrong?"

What do you know? What do you suspect?

She swallowed hard. "I-I…no?"

Oh drat, it came out as a question. As unbelievable as if she'd just tried to tell him a tall tale.

He frowned. "Tell me, love…"

She cringed at the cold way in which he said the endearment. Not at all with that kind, warm gentleness that actually made her feel…well, loved.

He tilted his head to the side to study her. "What became of that pin money I gave you?"

She blinked in surprise as her stomach sank. He knew.

She didn't know how, but he knew.

"I…I don't know what you mean."

"You asked me for money," he said as he stalked toward her.

"Which I happily gave to you. But you never did say what you needed it for."

She couldn't speak. Even if she had a lie at hand, she couldn't have blurted it out. She felt sick, her body cold all over. It didn't matter what she said because he knew.

She could see it in the set of his shoulders and the lack of warmth in his eyes. She could hear it in the hard suspicion that laced his tone.

Her stomach twisted and turned, her ribcage tightening as her foolish mind went blank. She couldn't think of a single excuse.

She couldn't even imagine how to begin to tell him the truth. Especially now, when he was staring at her with such mistrust.

He stopped just short of touching her, so she had to crane her neck to hold his gaze.

"Tell me, Madeline," he said.

Her heart clenched when she caught a flicker of pain behind that cold, hard mask. She didn't want to hurt him. She wrung her shaking hands together. More than anything, she did not want to hurt this man who'd been so good to her.

He stepped closer. "If I were to look, would I find more money missing?"

She didn't answer, but she supposed the tears of guilt and shame that rimmed her eyes gave her away.

"Why?" he rasped. "Why would you steal from me when you know I'd give you anything you ask?"

She shook her head. Foley. It was Foley who'd told him. That much was obvious. He was the only person who knew what she'd done. Indeed, he'd taken the pouch full of coins and given her an admonishment about how she ought to be quicker with her next payment.

But it was a lie, wasn't it? It wasn't about the money or how quickly she could get it.

It was about the countess wanting to destroy her and her happiness. It had always been about that.

Madeline's lips quivered as horror stole over her. She'd been a fool to think there was any other way out of this mess. Her mother would not rest until she was ruined. Until every bit of happiness was taken from her.

"Why, Madeline?" he said. "Just…tell me why."

But she couldn't. Because…how? How do you tell the man you're coming to love that he was not the first to see you naked? She wasn't sure she could say it aloud. She knew for certain she could not bear it if his gaze filled with betrayal. Or worse, disgust.

But betrayal was already there, wasn't it?

He was already backing away from her with disgust.

Imagine how he'd react if he knew the whole sordid truth. He'd think her just as wanton and wicked as his stepmother. She clapped a hand over her mouth, but she couldn't stop a sob.

Her mother had done this, and she'd done it on purpose.

Happiness would never be hers so long as the countess was there to destroy it.

His hands gripped her shoulders. "Tell me what's going on, Madeline. I am your husband. You ought to be able to tell me what's happening." His grip tightened, and there was no hiding the anguish in his eyes. It was anger mixed with hurt and…

She choked on another sob.

Hope.

He wanted to believe her.

He wanted to help her, even now after whatever Foley had said to him.

She took a step back. "My mother needed money."

"For what?" he snapped. "I'm already restoring their home and have offered assistance—"

"Not that," she said. "She wants…" *My downfall. She wants me ruined.* "She wants more money. She thinks…she thinks I owe it to her."

He shook his head. "The woman is just as mad as your father."

"No, she's not," she muttered miserably.

And that made it so much worse.

Their father had been cruel, of that there was no doubt. Even Albert hadn't been spared from their father's erratic temper and violent mood swings. The mad earl was vindictive and spiteful toward his own children. He'd gone into fits of rage over the slightest wrongdoing and then would spend days at a time happy as could be. It was the inconsistency of his nature that made others think him mad. It was his bizarre actions, like forcing his daughter to be imprisoned, that had likely had the servants whispering about his unhealthy state of mind.

But the thing about her father was…everyone knew him to be mad. There was a safety to his madness. *He's not in his right mind* became the excuse they gave him. It took some of the sting from his blows.

The countess was something different altogether.

"She's in her right mind, just…angry," Madeline continued.

She could feel his stare. But her thoughts were whirring about, muddling her senses, and making her stomach twist and churn with indecision.

Part of her wanted to tell him. Everything. All about her childhood. Her father. The woman they claimed to be her mother who hated her with a passion.

The ways her mother had tormented her as she got older, fueling her father's fears that Madeline would be raped or kidnapped unless locked away. Forbidding her brother to teach her and sending him off when he got old enough to stand up on her behalf.

"Why is she angry?" William demanded. A muscle ticked in his jaw.

He was only barely hanging onto his patience. And could she blame him?

She'd stolen from him. Lied to him. She'd planned to run away from him before they'd even wed.

"Madeline, talk to me," he said, dipping his head to meet her gaze. "I cannot help you if you do not tell me what's going on."

Her heart twisted. He still wanted to help her.

This man. This kind, loving man. He'd been so hurt in the past and yet he still had so much love to give.

"Is she holding something over you?" he asked. "Is your mother threatening you in some way?"

She didn't answer. She couldn't.

No matter what she said, he would think less of her. He would pull away from her.

She would lose him.

It would be her word versus her mother and Foley's. And right then and there, she saw the end.

She'd been a fool to think her story would end differently than it had begun. Only a romantic nitwit would imagine that she truly was living a fairy tale.

"I cannot tell you, I'm sorry," she said, backing away as tears threatened. "I can't tell you this."

But he'd learn of it. He'd find out.

Her mother's cruel smile flashed before her eyes. The smugness in Foley's features—before he'd gone and done what they'd said they wouldn't.

He'd told William. Maybe not everything, but enough.

Her mother was a cat and she the mouse. Was it about money? Yes. Perhaps. But it was so much more. No amount of stolen coin would assuage her mother's hatred for her.

No amount of appeasing her wishes would change the ending of Madeline's tale.

"She'll ruin this," she said. "She'll ruin me, and she will ruin you in the process."

"What?" He shook his head. "Madeline, what do you mean? Ruin what? How?"

She reached out for him as her chest felt like it was splitting in two. "I know you have no reason to, but please—please believe me that I would never willingly hurt you."

His gaze darted to her eyes, his expression one of hurt and confusion. "You want me to believe you, but you won't tell me anything."

She opened her mouth and shut it.

He took a step back, until her hands fell from his chest. "Madeline, tell me what is going on, or I'll have no choice but to find out for myself."

"William, please…"

"Please what?" he snapped.

Her mind raced with ways she could stop her mother before she did something unbearable…like spread rumors that would ruin her husband's reputation forever.

She would, that much Madeline now understood. She would make William out to be a cuckold and a fool in her quest to ensure that Madeline never found happiness.

But maybe she could stop her. If she could get to Albert…

Or no. No there was no time for that.

But she could leave. She could walk away now so William wouldn't be hurt because of her.

"Please what, Madeline?" he growled.

"Trust me," she whispered.

He laughed, the sound bitter and sharp. "Trust the woman who's just stolen from me. Who cannot be bothered to tell me why or to even attempt an explanation."

She bit her lip, tears burning.

"Fine," he snapped, walking away from her. "You leave me no other choice."

"William!"

But he ignored her shout as he stormed toward the bedroom door, throwing it open and slamming it shut behind him so hard it shook.

In the silence that followed, her heart crumbled, and her knees shook until she fell onto her bed.

All her life she'd been alone. Aside from Albert, she'd never had a single soul to call friend, let alone someone to love.

And now she had friends, and she'd found a man she loved with all her heart.

And yet…she'd never felt more alone.

CHAPTER SIXTEEN

AYDEN FELT LIKE a man possessed as he strode down the narrow alleyways that made up the area known as Vestry Lane.

"Are you sure you know what you're doing?" Malcolm asked.

"Yes." *No.* Of course, Hayden didn't know what he was doing. Did he look like a man with proper reasoning skills? He doubted it. He'd shown up on Malcolm's doorstep crazed with suspicions and fury.

The worst part was, he knew not where to direct his anger.

He didn't want to be angry with Madeline. He didn't want this nagging poisonous suspicion anywhere near their marriage. Everything in him wanted to believe her, to trust her...

But he couldn't. Only a fool would trust a woman who'd lied and stolen.

He stopped short, leaning forward to catch his breath and try to get his head on straight.

Malcolm stopped beside him, his arms crossed. "Hayden, you know better than to believe a word that swine Foley says."

Hayden straightened. "Indeed. I do." He threw his arms out wide. "But tell me. What am I to believe when my wife will not speak to me? When she goes behind my back, and...and..." He trailed off with a curse, looking away from the sympathy in Malcolm's eyes. "You wouldn't understand."

"Wouldn't I?" Malcolm's voice was level, but there was a hint of amusement there that had Hayden glancing over in question.

"Remind me to tell you the sordid tale of the way I met my wife," he said with a wry smile. "Actually, no. Forget that. Vivian would murder me. Just know that I understand what you're going through better than you know."

Hayden let out a huff of exasperation. "Then you know why I must confront Foley." He looked to the gaming hell, the exterior bland and nondescript, but the interior an extravagant shrine to vice, just like nearly every other seemingly benign townhome and shopfront on these seedy streets. "If Foley has the answers, I need to hear it."

"It'll be lies, every word out of his mouth," Malcolm said. "He's manipulating you, and you know it."

"Maybe. But it would be a start at least, wouldn't it?" He turned back to Malcolm with arched brows. "Clearly he and her mother are holding something over her." Something inside of him settled as he acknowledged that point. It was the one thought that gave him hope.

He'd meant it when he'd told her he could forgive and understand just about anything…if she were being honest.

"If they're blackmailing her or forcing her hand in some way, I need to know so I can help her."

"And if she's not the victim here?" Malcolm said quietly. "If she is indeed complicit in some way?"

"You don't believe that," Hayden said.

Malcolm shrugged. "It doesn't matter what I think. You are her husband. You are the one who needs to decide if you trust her or not. What if she is complicit in some way? I know you're thinking it. You wouldn't be here seeking answers if not."

Hayden's heart ached at the thought, and his jaw felt like it might shatter as the suspicions and jealousies he'd been trying to avoid speared him in the chest. He didn't want to believe it. He didn't even want to think it. But she'd left him no choice. If she'd only just spoken to him, offered some sort of explanation…

But she hadn't. And he would not fall for a woman's lies. He would not be made a fool by his own wife.

"If she's not innocent then…then I'd need to know that, too," he finally answered.

Malcolm said nothing, but his slight flinch gave him away.

"You think I'm wrong not to take her at her word."

"I didn't say that," he said. "If my wife were keeping secrets from me, it would drive me mad as well."

Mad. The word made him think of her father. The mad earl, everyone called him. Hayden could only imagine what she'd endured in her lifetime. With him for a father, and the countess as a mother… He nearly shuddered at the thought of the other woman. She'd spoken of her daughter like she was cattle to be bought and sold.

His poor wife had gone through so much.

"I want to believe her," Hayden said, the words plaintive. He felt like a child begging Malcolm to understand.

Malcolm nodded. "You have your reasons to find trust difficult. More than most, I'd imagine."

Hayden tensed at the inference to his mother and stepmother.

"But Benedict was right when he said that trust is a choice," Malcolm continued. "And it's one every man must make for himself when he enters into marriage."

Hayden looked away. "Maybe you're right," as he spoke, he began to walk toward the gaming hell again with renewed determination. "But I gave my wife a chance to explain, and she wouldn't."

"So, you're going to Foley for answers?" Malcolm called after him in disbelief.

"No," he said, slowing so Malcolm could catch up. "I'm going to Foley for information."

"Hayden—"

Hayden lifted a hand to cut him off, stopping short just in front of the gaming hell. "I'm not saying I'll believe a word he says. But innocent or not, my wife needs my help. And I cannot help her if I don't know what's going on."

Malcolm seemed to be stewing that over. "I don't know that this is the right way to go about it, old friend. You're not acting like yourself."

Hayden gave a huff of rueful amusement. "I haven't acted like myself since I found Madeline alone in that prison of a bedroom. I don't suppose there's any going back at this rate."

Malcolm chuckled. "Perhaps you're right. Even so…"

"Look, Malcolm, I brought you here in the event that this venture goes awry and I need a second," he said. "But if you'd rather turn around—"

"Don't be daft," Malcolm said. "Of course, I'm not going anywhere. Besides, we both know that you'll be safer on these streets if you're with me."

Hayden acknowledged this with a grunt. Everyone knew that Malcolm's bastard brother was the man best known as Beast on these streets. He was an enforcer for the mysterious and powerful man the locals called King, and everyone knew to steer clear of anyone linked to Beast. Even if the two men were far from friends, being his brother made Malcolm the safest man in this neighborhood.

"Come on then," Malcolm said with a sigh, leading the way past a guard at the door, who regarded them with a dark glare.

Inside, the air was thick with smoke and loud with raucous laughter. Whores draped themselves over the well-dressed gentlemen who gathered at tables near the back, mounds of coin heaped on the table before them.

Foley spotted them first and shouted over to them, his smile one of smug satisfaction. Almost as if he'd been expecting them.

"Little maggot," Malcolm muttered beside him.

"I honestly have no idea how he's stayed alive this long," Hayden said.

Together they made their way toward the weasel who was whispering in another man's ear. The fellow looked up from his cards with a start. The man was unfamiliar to Hayden, but he was dressed well enough. He had a thick, well-oiled mustache and beard, and a cigar dangled from his lips. But it was the predatory look in his eyes that made Hayden's gut clench with wariness.

"Birds of a feather," Malcolm muttered as they drew closer.

Hayden grunted his agreement. The bearded man stood and towered over Foley, but there was something disgustingly similar in their demeanors. It was cruelty mixed with triumph.

Whatever they were up to, they clearly thought they held the upper hand.

The thought that either man had anything to do with Madeline made him temporarily overwhelmed with fury. His steps faltered.

"You all right?" Malcolm asked.

"I will kill him," he growled. "I will murder them both."

Malcolm put a hand on his shoulder with a weary sigh. "And this, right here, was why I'd thought it best to wait until you had your emotions under control."

Hayden shrugged him off as the two men headed toward them. "I'll never have control of my emotions where Madeline is concerned."

Malcolm glanced at him in surprise at the admission. But what was the point in denying it? His life had been upended the moment he'd met her. Everything he'd thought was important was flipped on its head. His freedom? His independence? Bah! They'd paled in comparison to having someone to take care of. And then he'd gotten to know her, and it was suddenly impossible to imagine what life had been like before her.

And now…

Hell, now he couldn't begin to imagine what life would be like if he lost her.

"I had a feeling you'd come," Foley said, his lips curved in a sneer. "Not too good to address me now, are you, Lord Hayden?"

Hayden ignored him. He'd learned long ago that this was the best way to infuriate a sycophantic little arse like Foley, who wanted nothing more than to prove himself a man.

"Who are you?" he said to the bearded man.

"Name's Mr. Percer, my lord." His smile was insinuating and left Hayden feeling queasy.

"Percer. Just what do you have to do with the lies this jackass was spouting to me earlier?"

"I beg your pardon," Foley sputtered. "I came to you in good faith to tell you what sort of woman you'd wed."

Hayden reached out and snatched the pissant up by his neck, choking him until he turned red.

It was a testament to the sort of establishment King ran that not a soul stopped what he was doing to pay any attention.

"Careful what you say about my wife, Foley," Hayden said, his voice low and calm despite the way his blood boiled with rage. "She is a marchioness and anything you say against her you will pay for with your life."

"My lord, I assure you," Percer started, his hands up and his gaze maddeningly innocent. "Foley and I only want to spare you humiliation in the future. Indeed," his smile was sickeningly triumphant, "I do believe you'll be indebted to me for my honesty once you've heard what I have to say."

The man toyed with his mustache, feigning humility so poorly that Malcolm muttered an exasperated oath beside Hayden.

"You may even wish to support my business once you've learned the embarrassment I could spare you and your…wife."

The derisive tone he used to say "wife" left Hayden shaking with rage, and he let his hand drop from Foley's neck.

"It's money he's after," Malcolm murmured, derision clear in his voice. "Another attempt at extortion, I'd guess."

Hayden's eyes narrowed on the bearded man. "Speak now before I kill you," he growled.

The man's eyes flared wide, and he looked to Malcolm who shrugged. "He may just kill you anyway. You're an awfully unlikeable fellow. I'd speak if I were you."

"Yes, well…" He cleared his throat. "You must know we are

trying to look out for your best interests, Lord Hayden."

"Of course," Foley said, rubbing his neck. "The countess herself asked that we convey this information. She did not wish for you to be saddled with her wayward daughter without knowing the truth of her character or the extent of what she'd done to get herself locked up in that tower."

Hayden seethed with fury, but behind that pounding rush of anger, he knew he needed to hear this. Whatever lies they were about to spew.

And they were lies. He knew that, too.

He trusted her that much.

The thought was a punch to his gut. He trusted her. He did trust her. But he forced his attention back to the men. "Tell me then."

"You see, sir, the rumors about her being locked in that tower were true. But not for the reason you believe," Foley said. "The countess did it for the girl's own good. To keep her from ruining herself. You see, the girl has a..." he glanced over at Percer, who looked grim, "a penchant, you might say. She inherited her father's wicked urges, you see..."

He looked to Percer again, and the man dipped his head in a poor imitation of humility and embarrassment. "I didn't know she was meant to marry another, you see—"

"Say it," Hayden growled.

Say whatever slander you have in mind and be done with it.

"Well, I'll just say this...." Percer arched his brows meaningfully. "Man to man, you know." He leaned forward. "That birthmark is in just the right location, isn't it? Looks like a map to the holy land, if you know what I mean."

Hayden's mind flashed on the birthmark on his wife's thigh. His blood ran cold even as his mind scrambled to justify this man's knowledge of his wife's body. Her mother told him or...or...

His mind went blank as the men kept talking.

He barely knew what they said. And it didn't matter. None of it mattered. For in that moment, he knew the truth. He didn't need an explanation.

He knew not how this man was aware of his wife's body; he only knew that his wife was innocent. She'd been a victim all her life, and these men meant to make a victim of her now.

Rage the likes of which he'd never known gave him an unearthly sense of calm. It all seemed so simple and so clear.

He trusted his wife.

He loved his wife.

And he would happily kill any man who set out to harm her.

"Meet me at dawn," he said to Percer.

"What?" The other man sputtered, his face going red. "I'm trying to help you, my lord—"

"By spreading lies about my wife? I think not. I'll see you at dawn. You choose the weapon."

CHAPTER SEVENTEEN

MADELINE ANSWERED THE front door herself, even though the sun hadn't even yet begun to rise.

Why rouse any of the servants when she'd never gone to sleep?

For hours she'd paced the lower floor, waiting for her husband to return.

She threw open the door, expecting…what? She wasn't certain. Her husband wouldn't knock on his own door.

But she hadn't expected to find Vivian on her doorstep, unkempt and visibly exhausted like she, too, hadn't slept a wink.

"Vivian?"

"I'm sorry to intrude, dear, it's just…"

Madeline didn't give her a chance to finish before she pulled her inside and wrapped her arms around her friend. "Oh, Vivian, I'm so grateful you're here."

"I'm afraid you won't be once you hear my news," Vivian warned.

When Madeline backed away with a sniff, her blood ran cold with fear. "What is it? Is it Hayden? Is he hurt?"

"No. Or…not yet, at least."

Madeline's hands were shaking when she went to cover her mouth a moment later after Vivian stopped speaking.

"A duel? When? Where?" She was already rushing toward the

door. "I must stop him."

"Madeline, you can't. Malcolm tried. As did I when they got to our house to prepare."

"To prepare. But…" Her stomach dropped as her head swam. "Oh, Vivian, he mustn't."

Vivian shook her head, looking nearly as distressed as Madeline felt. "I'm afraid he feels he must. He says that this man was telling lies about you."

"Who? Foley?" She could only imagine what that man had said. But she feared none of it was lies.

"Mr. Percer." Vivian shrugged. "I've never heard of him."

Madeline stilled but the world seemed to spin around her. Her hands went to her belly as her insides heaved. "Oh Lord, what did he say?"

She could imagine. And with what Foley had said to her before… The way he'd made it sound like she'd wanted to be touched…

A cold sweat broke out on her forehead as she swayed.

Hayden must despise her.

A searing pain struck her behind her ribcage, as if her heart were being pierced in two. It had been too good to last. Deep down she'd known it would end. But the thought of something happening to Hayden. Of him being hurt or worse, and all because of her lies and secrets…

"Here. Have a seat." Vivian took Madeline by the arm and guided her to the parlor.

"My lady!" The housekeeper entered, looking startled. "Whyever are you awake? And you have guests. Oh, dear me—"

"It's quite all right," Vivian said. "I showed up unannounced at an ungodly hour. But I wonder, could you make some tea for us? I'm afraid Lady Hayden is not feeling well."

"Why, yes, of course," she said, hurrying out the way she'd come in.

Both women were quiet until she was out of earshot.

"I take it you're familiar with this man," Vivian said slowly, her tone gentle.

"Yes, but it's not…it's not what he says. It's not…oh, what must Hayden think of me."

Vivian gave her a sympathetic wince. "Dear, it seems *all* Hayden is thinking about is you. He believes he's protecting you from whatever vile accusations this man made."

"But that's just it…" Madeline plucked at the fabric of her night-rail, her eyes too wet with tears to see her own hands. "It's not all lies. And…and…I should have told him." She broke down crying then, and when the housekeeper returned with tea, she found Madeline curled up weeping in Vivian's lap like a child.

"There now," Vivian said when the housekeeper quietly departed again. "He'll be fine, and you and Hayden will sort it all out."

"But you don't know what I've done." She sniffed, sitting up.

"Did you have a tryst with this man?" Vivian asked.

"No. No, of course not."

Vivian's brows drew together with sympathy. "Was there a man before Hayden? One you loved, perhaps?"

"No! There was never anyone for me but Hayden. He is everything to me. He's…" She stopped short. These were words she ought to say to her husband. This was what she should have said last night when he'd confronted her. "Oh, Vivian, I've made such a mess of everything."

"There, there," Vivian said as she stroked her back. "It will all come out right in the end. Duels these days aren't what they used to be, you know. No one will come to any real harm, I guarantee it."

Madeline nodded. But until she had Hayden back here safe and sound in her arms, she couldn't bring herself to believe it. They sat in silence for a long while. "So now we just…wait?"

Vivian sighed. "I'm afraid so."

"You do not have to…that is, you must be tired and—"

Vivian's snort of rueful amusement cut her off. "Madeline, I am not leaving you until Hayden walks through those doors and apologizes for scaring you so."

Madeline sniffled, gratitude swelling in her chest.

"You and the others, you've all been so kind to me," she said quietly as she reached for Vivian's hands. "Thank you."

Vivian smiled gently. "It's called being a friend. And we are happy to count you as one."

Madeline's throat grew tight with another wave of emotion. "I've never had friends, but also…I've never felt this before. What I feel for my husband."

Vivian's lips quirked. "It's called love, dear."

Madeline's eyes welled up all over again. "It's dreadful."

Vivian burst out laughing. "It can be. But it can also be the most wonderful thing in the world."

Madeline nodded. "Yes. I've experienced that as well, I suppose." She felt warmth surge through her at the memory of her husband's arms around her. Of that tender gleam in his eyes when he was smiling down at her.

"He's been so patient and so kind," she said. "I never imagined there was a man like William out there in the world. At first, he'd seemed too good to be true. I think some part of me was waiting for something bad to happen. To discover that he wasn't as good as he seemed."

"But that never happened," Vivian guessed.

Madeline sniffed. "Time and again he's proved that he's even better than I'd first imagined. He's human, of course. He has his flaws and mistakes, but his heart is so very good."

Her throat grew choked as she stared out the window, watching the sky grow brighter. "The only person I've ever trusted and relied on was my brother, Albert. But he's been gone for so long now." She turned to Vivian. "It's not his fault. Whenever he returns to London, he visits me and he's wonderful, but… I suppose what I'm trying to say is… I don't know how to rely on others. All my husband wanted was for me to trust him and…and I didn't."

"Oh Madeline," Vivian said as she squeezed her hand. "Trust

doesn't come easily for anyone, but for those of us who've been mistreated…"

Madeline glanced over in surprise. "You?"

Vivian nodded. "My first husband wasn't nearly as kind and wonderful as my Malcolm."

Madeline felt a wave of emotion on her friend's behalf. "I'm glad you found him."

"We found each other," she corrected. "And it took time and work on both our parts to overcome our pasts and to begin to forge our future."

Madeline nodded. "I just hope that I have time with William. I hope…" She bit her lip as her mind rushed to call up her worst fear. "I hope I have the chance to explain."

"Explain what, my dear?" William's voice in the doorway had her gasping with surprise before she shot up out of her seat to race over to her husband.

He held his arms out and caught her when she threw herself against him. Tears trailed down her cheeks as his arms wrapped around her waist, so tightly that when he straightened, she was lifted off the ground, her toes dangling above the floor as she burrowed her face in his neck.

"You're here," she sobbed against his chest. "You're all right."

"Shh," he hushed. "There's no need to cry, my love. I'm fit as a fiddle."

"And the other man?" Vivian asked.

Malcolm responded as he crossed the room to join her. "Never showed. The coward sent a servant to tell us he was en route to the continent."

"For business," Hayden said, his tone dry as he rubbed Madeline's back.

She couldn't tear herself away from him. His scent, his warmth, his voice…it was all so wonderfully dear.

And she could have lost him.

"Darling, please don't cry," he murmured. "I'm well, and that bastard Percer is gone from the country."

"Never to return if he knows what's good for him," Malcolm said.

"Come, my dear," Vivian said as she tucked her hand in Malcolm's elbow. "We should both get some rest and let these two have their privacy."

Malcolm clapped Hayden on the back on his way out, and Vivian called her farewells, but Madeline couldn't bring herself to lift her head from her husband's shoulder.

They could hear the front door close behind them, and even still, she stayed where she was, burrowing into him as if sheer proximity could keep him in her life and out of danger.

With a sigh, he readjusted her, bending down so he could scoop her up into his arms. "Love, have you been awake and fretting all night?"

She nodded. She was shaking now. Trembling like a leaf as she realized just how easily she could have lost him.

"And it would have been my fault," she babbled aloud.

He sank down onto the settee and arranged her on his lap, still holding her close and comforting her. "What was your fault?"

She pulled back finally to look at him. "It's all my fault, William. I should have told you everything. I should have trusted you."

He nodded slowly, his gaze more serious than she'd ever seen it. "Perhaps. And perhaps I should have trusted you, too. Maybe I should have given you more time or—"

"No," she said with a sniff. "You were right. How could I expect you to believe in me when I didn't trust you and..."

He leaned forward when she trailed off, pressing his forehead to hers as he gave her a gentle smile. "And perhaps we're both to blame, hmm? Or, better yet, perhaps we can both just learn from this and move forward." He leaned back to arch his brows. "What do you say?"

Happiness hit her in the chest like a cannonball, slamming into her so hard she was temporarily breathless. A noise escaped her that was somewhere between a sob and a laugh.

He smiled in response.

"You are wonderful, do you know that?" she asked.

His grin broadened. "I have my moments."

She choked on a laugh as she leaned forward to kiss him. He caught her close, his lips hungry as they met hers. His tongue flicked out to taste her, and she opened for him with a moan.

"My wife," he growled as he held her close, their bodies melting into one another as if they were made to be joined.

She could feel his member swelling beneath her bottom, and her whole body grew tight and heavy in response. She wanted nothing more than to take him inside her. To lose herself in the feel of him.

"Wait," she said. "You…we…we must talk first. I don't want any more time to pass with secrets between us."

His head fell back with a groan. "You're right, of course."

He reached for her hands and squeezed as he gazed up at her from beneath heavy lids. "And I don't want another moment to pass in this marriage in which we are anything less than honest with one another."

She nodded. "Yes, William."

He shifted her to his side, allaying temptation. "Tell me," he said. "Tell me everything. I will not judge you, Madeline. I believe that what you tell me is the truth. But I need you to trust me with that truth."

She pressed her lips together, overcome with emotion at the pleading in his eyes. "You…you'll believe me even though…"

His brows drew down, and she caught a hint of his anguish. "The things he said, love." He glanced down at her body. "The things he knew…" He drew in a deep breath. "It killed me to hear him speak of you like that. It hurt even more that you didn't tell me your secrets yourself. But, sweetheart…"

He reached out and touched her cheek. "I knew right then and there how much I do trust you. It took that man's filthy lies for me to see the truth. I didn't need your explanations to know that whatever your history with that man and Foley and your mother—you are my wonderful, sweet, loyal wife."

She started to cry again, swiping at the tears as her heart melted.

"I know you. Even if I don't know your secrets, I know *you*," he said. "I know you…and I love you."

CHAPTER EIGHTEEN

LISTENING TO MADELINE'S tale was torture.

It took everything Hayden had not to excuse himself so he could run off and murder her mother. And her father. And Foley, though it was well established that man should have been put out of his misery months ago.

But he didn't move except to pull Madeline close and hold her as she shook in his arms as she recounted first her miserable childhood trapped in that home. It seemed her father was overprotective to an extreme on the best of days. On his bad days, he'd been paranoid and cruel. The brother hadn't had it easy, by the sounds of it, but his illegitimate daughter had suffered most of all.

The brother at least had a mother who—if not loved him the way a mother ought—supported him. As the heir and her legitimate son, she'd favored him.

"It's not Albert's fault," she said when she caught a look at his features.

He kept silent.

He supposed her brother had done what he could for her, but that did not excuse the way he'd left her there these past two years. Coming to visit, perhaps, but setting off again and again to obey his mother's orders, leaving Madeline alone and imprisoned.

Hayden stroked her hair, holding her head to his chest as she wrapped her arms around his waist. He kissed the top of her hair. "Love, what happened with this Percer man?"

He felt her stiffen, but she lifted her head. "I don't want to tell you."

His heart twisted, but not because he doubted her. He knew now that Benedict had been right. Trust wasn't something you could reason your way into. It was based on faith. But his heart ached all the same at the pain in her eyes.

He would happily kill whoever had put that pain there.

"You don't have to tell me this morning if you don't wish," he started.

"No. No, I have to. It's just...I don't want you to see me differently."

He cupped her face in his hands. "When I look upon you, I will only ever see the woman I love."

Her smile was watery but genuine. But then it fell, and her gaze darted away. "My mother realized that the earldom was facing ruin. My brother has been trying to salvage the situation these past two years since he came of age, but with Father still alive and Mother's control over him and the household..." She shook her head. "Anyway, she's never worried about the earldom or its legacy. Only her own future. She was terrified of being poor. Of what would happen to her when Father dies..."

She bit her lip and shook her head. "She treated Albert better than me, but I don't think she's capable of love. Maybe she was before...before Father. Perhaps his cruelty made her hard." Madeline shrugged. "Or maybe Father chose to marry her because she was ruthless. I don't know."

He stroked a thumb over her cheek. "What did she do, love?"

"This last time when she sent Albert away, I knew...I knew she had something planned. But I'd never guessed..." She visibly swallowed and licked her lips. "She meant to...to sell me."

He went rigid beneath her weight but fought for control as he stroked her back. "Sell you how, love?"

"Suddenly Foley was a presence in our house, and it soon

became clear that he was her…go-between, I suppose. He was spreading the word to wealthy men that the mad earl had a virgin daughter for the taking."

Rage had his muscles tensing, his jaw clenching. He didn't trust himself to speak. Her fingers toyed with a button on his coat, her gaze riveted on his chest.

If he were to speak now with all the anger he was feeling, he was afraid she'd clam up for good.

"Percer was one of them," she said. "I heard my mother talking. She even gloated to me once about how much these men would pay to be the ones to claim my virginity."

"She was going to turn you into a whore," he said, the words sputtering out in his shock and rage.

"Yes." She lifted her gaze. "My father is so far gone, you see. She could have told him I'd run away or…" She shrugged. "She could have claimed I'd died, I suppose. And Albert…"

She swallowed hard again, and he felt his ribcage crushing his heart at the pain in her features. "Well, that was why she was so forceful about sending him away. By the time he returned, he would have been too late to save me."

"I will kill her." The words slipped out in a harsh whisper. A promise. A vow.

To his surprise, she smiled up at him even though her eyes were rimmed with tears. "No. You won't. For you are no murderer."

He opened his mouth to protest, but she carried on with her sordid tale.

"The night you arrived so gracefully in my bedroom…" She shot him a wry smile that did nothing to hide the wariness in her eyes.

He reached for her hand and squeezed it. "You can tell me anything, love. I want to know it all so I can help to carry your burdens."

Her lips quivered. "It turns out there are a fair number of wealthy men with…dark appetites. So many that my mother decided to hold an auction."

"An auction?" He clamped his mouth shut at her wince. "Sorry. Go on."

"These gentlemen arrived at our house, and my mother brought me into this room to…to parade in front of them—"

His curse cut her off. "Like a damned animal," he spit out.

She nodded. "Yes, but then. They wanted to…to see more…and then they were…" She squeezed her eyes shut. "Then they were touching me and—"

"Sweetheart," he groaned, pulling her against him.

Her eyes flew open. "I did not…I never…I was a virgin when we wed."

Her gaze was so full of pleading that it very nearly broke his heart. "I know, love. But even if you weren't, you did nothing wrong."

He kissed her as if that could make her see. But she shook her head. "I didn't fight, though. I should have fought."

"You didn't fight because you were frightened and outnumbered and…" He caught her chin in his hand, forcing her to meet his gaze. "I hate your mother and those men for what they did to you. And I swear, I will make them pay. Every one of them."

She tried to look away, but he held her still.

"But Madeline, my love, you did nothing wrong. You were the victim of cruelty and those men's sick perversions. You are not to blame."

She bit her lip, the tears welling in her eyes and then spilling over.

"You said you were worried about how I would look at you when I knew the truth," he said, his voice low and gruff with emotions. "Well, look into my eyes and tell me what you see."

She did look. Her breathing hitched and her eyes widened as she truly looked into his eyes. Her brows drew together as her expression crumpled, the tears flowing freely as she drew in a shaky breath. Leaning forward, she pressed her lips to his, and he kissed her for so long and so thoroughly, he could taste the salt of her tears.

When she pulled back, she whispered, "I love you, too, William. I love you so very much."

The words rippled through him, and a groan was torn from deep down inside him. His arms came around her as he pulled her closer still. He hadn't realized how much he wanted and needed to hear those words until they passed her lips.

He crushed her to him, his face buried in her hair, against her neck, kissing her shoulder. "I love you," he said again and again. "I love you, and I will never walk away from you again."

She clung to him just as fiercely. "And I will never keep secrets from you."

He slid a hand beneath her knees. "Come upstairs with me, love. Let me show you how much I adore you."

She was already kissing him as he scooped her into his arms. The trek to their bedroom felt like an eternity as she teased him with kisses, her fingers restless in his hair and moving over the muscles of his chest and arms.

When he set her down on the bed, he took a moment to stand back and admire her, this strong, courageous beauty in his bed.

"What?" she asked with a small smile. "Why are you staring at me like that?"

He shook his head. "Just marveling at my good fortune."

She started to laugh. "I'm the one who ought to be marveling. If you hadn't come along that night..." She trailed off with a shake of her head, and he knelt beside her on the bed.

He kissed her gently. "Until I met you, I'd never believed in love. I thought it was a thing of fiction. And I certainly didn't believe in fate or destiny."

She reached up for him. "And now?"

He leaned over her, his nose brushing against hers. "Now I know that I was wrong. I was meant to find you that night."

She smiled, her eyes shining with love and affection. "Well, until I met you, *I* never believed that a happy ending was in store for me," she said. "But everything changed that night."

He leaned down until his chest was pressing against her, his swollen shaft fitting perfectly in that soft, welcoming heat between her thighs.

She parted her legs for him readily, her hips arching as she ground herself against him.

"And to think," he teased as he dipped his head to kiss her neck. "My friends thought me a fool for all those nights drinking and taking ridiculous risks."

"But now we know better," she said, laughter in her voice.

"That's right." He flicked open the buttons along her bodice, his lips covering each new area of exposed skin. "All that time I was just searching for you." He lifted his head with a grin. "I just didn't know it."

Her laughter was light and sweet, and he could have sworn he felt it warm him through like sunshine.

"And now I am the most happily married man," he said, using his nose to nudge aside the fabric of her nightdress so he could trail his lips over the soft, smooth skin of her breasts.

She gasped when his lips found her puckered nipple. Then he licked it, flicking it with his tongue until she whimpered, her fingers digging into his shoulders and upper back. When he drew the hardened peak into his mouth and suckled, she moaned, her hips bucking upward in invitation.

"Oh, my love," he said with a grin as he slid upward to capture her mouth in a lazy, hot kiss that left them both panting. "Now that I know just how badly you were mistreated, I'm going to make it my mission in life to replace every bad memory with good ones."

She groaned and writhed beneath him. "You already have."

He shook his head. "Oh, no, my sweet wife. Not yet." He moved back down to begin a slow trail of kisses. "I mean to kiss every inch of you. To make sure you know that there is no shame here with me. Your body is heaven on earth. It's meant to be treasured and adored." He glanced up as he moved his mouth down between her breasts, pressing gentle kisses to her belly. "*You* are meant to be treasured and adored, my love."

Her eyes glinted with emotion as she ran her fingers through his hair, cradling his head. "You deserve the same, you know. The fact that you believed me and trusted me even when I did not tell you my secrets…" She smiled down at him. "You were already my knight in shining armor for rescuing me the way you did. But now…" She moaned when his lips moved lower, finding that birthmark just above her curls. "But now you are truly my hero. I want everything with you. Love. Children. Happiness."

"Not a hero," he corrected. His grin was wicked as he spread her thighs wide and gazed down with hungry eyes at her wet folds. "Your husband. And I will give you anything you ask for."

CHAPTER NINETEEN

HAYDEN'S SWEET WIFE might have only asked for love, children, and happiness, but he meant to give her that and so much more.

Namely, vengeance.

Nearly a fortnight had passed since that ill-fated duel, and Hayden's nerves were on edge with impatience.

Or perhaps that was the musicians preparing for tonight's ball. Their constant starting and stopping as they rehearsed in the ballroom was enough to drive a man mad. The news that Malcolm had just delivered had him on edge, as well. It wasn't bad news, not in the least, but it had him rethinking what he thought he knew of his wife's brother and how this would play into his plans.

"She's here," Madeline said from the doorway of his study.

He turned to face her, his gorgeous wife with the kindest smile he'd ever known. "I'm coming with you," he said.

"It's not necessary, you know. The countess can't hurt me any longer."

He gave a little huff. He couldn't deny that. He and his friends had acted swiftly to ensure Madeline's mother, father, and those bloody arses who'd taken part in her mother's scheme were brought to justice.

Their first act had been to send Foley into exile. Raff and

Benedict had happily taken the lead on that front, as both had reasons to despise the cowardly knave. His father hadn't tried to defend him, nor his elder brother. The family seemed to know as well as anyone that the man was weak of character and evil of spirit. And so, no one had given Foley a penny before sending him off to America.

Hayden would be surprised if he lasted a day let alone years on his own in a foreign country.

But he was gone now, and Hayden had taken pleasure in tracking down Percer and the other men Foley had ratted out. All the men who'd been there that night had been ruined, financially and within society.

The only one left to punish was Madeline's mother. *Adopted* mother, she now liked to point out. He'd wanted to haul that woman into a deep lake with boulders tied to her ankles, but Madeline had asked to be the one to deal with her.

And so, he knew that he had to let her. Frustrating as that might be. But he didn't just trust his wife, he believed in her. Every day he saw just how strong she was. For it took more strength than he could imagine to not only survive all the cruelty she'd lived through but to still hold onto her kindness as well.

It was that which worried him now. "Just promise me that you won't go easy on her," he said. "Even if she cries."

Madeline laughed softly. "I promise you I will not undo all your work in making her powerless, no matter how much she cries." She made a face. "Though frankly, I cannot imagine her shedding a tear."

He gave her a lopsided grin as he strode toward her. "Let's find out then, shall we?"

She arched a brow, and he held his hands up in surrender. "I'll stay quiet, I promise. She is all yours to deal with."

Madeline smiled and turned to lead the way.

They found the countess waiting in his study. She was standing, her features pinched and her eyes filled with malice. She ignored her daughter and looked to him. "What is the meaning of this? One does not summon a countess—"

"Silence, Mother," Madeline spoke calmly. Almost…sweetly. And Hayden ignored the older woman to watch his exquisite wife.

Placidly, she placed her hands in front of her, clasping them together. Her white knuckles were the only sign that she wasn't quite as calm as she seemed.

"What is the meaning of—"

"You will listen to me for once," Madeline interjected, cutting the countess off succinctly. "My husband and his friends know, Mother. They know everything."

The countess's mouth opened and shut, indignation in her expression but the start of panic in her eyes.

Good. Hayden crossed his arms with satisfaction. Very good.

"They know everything you have done to me. They know about Father's health, mental and physical. They know that you had planned to sell me off to the highest bidder."

"I never!" she started, the countess's gaze flying to Hayden as if he might believe her.

"I said silence, Mother," Madeline said, her voice stern even though the countess was still looking at him pleadingly.

He arched his brows, his smile broadening. "I'd do what she says if I were you, Lady Ashburn. My wife holds all the power here, you know. Most definitely over you." He turned his smile on his wife. "And I'm not ashamed to admit over me, as well. She's really quite persuasive, you know."

Madeline's lips twitched with amusement at his teasing. But then she turned back to the countess. "The men have been dealt with," she said. "There is no money to be found there. You are finished, Mother. You and Father will be sent to the north to live in one of Father's dilapidated old estates alone. If you should try to come back to London, you will be imprisoned for your crimes. If you should start any rumors or try in any way to hurt me, my husband, Albert, or my friends, you will be punished according-ly."

The countess blanched, and Hayden's chest swelled with pride.

Not so much as a quiver in his wife's voice. His wife was strong, and she was only just beginning to realize how much so.

Madeline started to turn, dismissing her adopted mother without so much as a farewell.

"You cannot do this, you little ingrate."

"She can," he said simply. "And she has. In fact, it's already been done."

Madeline looked at him with a question in her eyes, and he directed the next part to her, since he hadn't yet had a chance to tell her of what Malcolm had just informed him.

"We've been working to track down Madeline's brother," he said. "And we found him."

Madeline's eyes lit with pleasure. "You found Albert?"

"It took a while because we'd been looking in the wrong places." He turned to the countess. The vengeful part of him wanted to see her reaction. "You see, while you'd been sending your son off to try and restore the funds to your failing earldom, your son had been doing his best to save Madeline from you and her father."

Madeline gasped. "What do you mean?"

He turned to her with a smile. "Yes, my love. It seems you were right, and I was wrong to ever doubt him. He does love you and was trying his best to save you. I just got to you first."

"My son would never betray me or his father," the countess started.

"Wouldn't he?" Madeline said, her voice cold as ice. "And why not? Neither of you ever showed him love, and much as you tried to keep us apart, we only ever had each other. So why do you think his loyalty would be to you?"

"Excellent point she makes, isn't it?" he murmured.

The countess sneered at him, but both he and Madeline ignored her.

"Where has he been?" she asked.

"It seems he's been trying to petition for guardianship, but he had to go about it carefully so word would not get back to your parents."

Madeline's eyes gleamed with pride. "I knew he hadn't abandoned me."

Hayden smiled. "I look forward to meeting him when he arrives."

"He's coming here?"

"Of course. Once Malcolm discovered his whereabouts, he sent for him. He gave him the message that you are out of danger and that…" here he spared another glance at the countess, "and that we have petitioned the crown to give him full control of the estate and its funds, considering your father's failing health."

"You cannot—" the countess started.

"We can and we have," Madeline said. "Now, if you please, Mother. We're hosting a ball tonight, and you are very much not welcome."

Hayden signaled to a footman who'd been waiting by the door.

"Thomas here will see you out," Hayden said. "And he has orders to use force if you resist."

"You cannot do this!" The countess was still shouting as his wife took his proffered arm and they left her behind, the door shutting with a click that muffled her shouts.

"How do you feel, love?" he asked.

She grinned up at him. "Like I am the luckiest lady in the land."

He leaned down to kiss her, and she wrapped her arms around his neck.

"I cannot believe the nightmare is over."

He scowled teasingly at the ballroom, where music played loudly. "And just in time for the next nightmare to begin."

"Oh stop," she laughed. "I know you do not enjoy balls, but at least we'll get to dance together."

"Mmph. That's the only part I'm looking forward to." He

drew her back into his arms. "Well, that and seeing all the looks of admiration and envy on our guests' faces when they see my wonderful wife in all her glory."

She laughed, slapping his shoulder lightly. "You tease."

"I don't. You will be the envy of them all."

She laughed harder, and she opened her mouth to protest but was cut off by the butler who turned the corner. "Ah, my lady. Forgive me for the interruption but your visitors have begun to arrive."

Madeline's face split with a grin. "That must be our friends. Philippa, Evangeline, and Vivian all insisted on arriving early to ensure I had all the moral support I could endure for my first hostessing event."

"You don't need their support," he said.

"I know that, but don't tell them," she shot back with a wink. "They like to feel useful."

His head fell back with a laugh. "Very well. In that case, let us go greet our friends and prepare for your big night."

He wrapped an arm around her waist. "I'm proud of you, love."

She leaned into him with a sigh. "Thank you, William." She glanced up with a grin. "Now come along. We need to toast with our friends."

"And what are we toasting to?"

She glanced back at where they'd left the countess. "To the end of one chapter…"

He kissed the top of her head as he finished, "And to all the new beginnings."

About the Author

Bella Moxie is the author of the steamy regency romance series, *Dukes Gone Dirty*, as well as the offshoot novella series, *Rogues Gone Dirty*. Her books are spicy, but filled with sweet, satisfying, over-the-top love that not even the most alpha hero can resist.

Grab a free, steamy regency romance novella when you join Bella's newsletter at:
eepurl.com/gW_QWL